The vampire stared down at the wood in his chest and let out a loud, degrading laugh.

"You've got to use more force than that if you want to kill someone." He yanked the wood out and dropped it to the ground. The expression on his face said he didn't find her to be a threat at all. He thought she was an inferior being. He'd proven that by letting her attempt to stake him, knowing full well she would never be able to kill him.

His fingers twitched as if he was thinking about snapping her neck, but he paused and glanced at the fight going on over her shoulder, which apparently looked like more of a challenge. "I'll deal with you later," he promised, his gaze returning to Bradley, "but right now, I'm going to kill your boyfriend." Grabbing her shoulder, he shoved her roughly to the pavement.

Bradley hit the ground and was barely able to keep her skull from connecting with the concrete. Rocks dug viciously into her palms, embedding themselves in her skin. She didn't stop to examine them, though. These men were about to kill her and Beau. She couldn't afford to tend to her wounds. Staggering to her feet, she closed her fist around the make-shift stake she'd been given and started in Beau's direction.

Two men had Beau pinned to the ground and the vampire that had been holding her was ramming his boot down into his gut. They were all bent over and didn't see Bradley coming...or perhaps they simply didn't care.

She reached the group and stood directly behind the vampire that had tossed her to the ground. Lifting her arms over her head, she brought the shattered piece of baseball bat down as hard as she could.

The wood went nearly through the vampire's body. In shock, he attempted to straighten so he could turn and face his attacker. His movements helped drive the stake the rest of the way through his heart.

Bradley saw his startled, wide eyes before he turned to dust. She stumbled backwards in horror, her arms aching with the effort she'd used to kill the vampire. Before what she'd just done could fully sink in, arms wrapped around her from behind, pinning her arms to her sides. There was a feral growl and she could see fangs out of the corner of her eye.

On the ground, one of the men holding Beau down released his arm in surprise when his fellow henchman turned to dust.

As the body disintegrated, the stake fell through the dust. Beau caught it with his free hand and swiftly slammed it upward through the startled vampire's chest. "Two vampires, one werewolf," he said to himself, obviously liking those odds much better.

Before the vampire was even done turning to dust, Beau reached above his head, stretching to the tree he'd been tied to earlier. He grabbed onto the chain that had been used to restrain him. Sitting up, he seized the other man holding him down. Beau swiftly wrapped the chain around his neck, tightening it to crush the other man's windpipe.

The arms around Bradley jarred her around, but she still saw Beau snap the man's neck with the chain.

The man's head lulled lifelessly to the side, his eyes glazing over.

"Nice knowing you, Arliss," Beau jeered.

There were only the two vampires left now. One was a few feet in front of Beau and the other was holding Bradley.

Beau looked around thoughtfully. "I see Kelvin didn't return for this. Too scared to die with the rest of you?"

Enraged at Beau's comment and the sight of Arliss being down, the vampire near Beau rushed at him.

While the two of them began exchanging blows, the vampire holding Bradley began to drag her toward a car.

Bradley kicked and struggled against him. Somehow, she knew that if he got her into that car, she was dead. They would torture her to find out what they wanted, and then they would kill her. She wasn't stopping him with her resistance, though. He was too big, too strong.

"Beau!" she screamed in horror. She twisted violently in her assailant's arms, trying to loosen his grip on her. "Beau!" She pushed her feet off the ground, kicking them wildly in the air and forcing all of her weight onto the vampire. She knocked him off balance, nearly dragging him to the ground with the sudden movement.

"Quit struggling!" he snarled.

He had her nearly to the car when, in a last ditch effort, Bradley threw her head back, hitting him in the face. She felt fangs sink into the back of her head, stinging her flesh, but at least he dropped her. Breathing raggedly from the effort used to get free, Bradley started to crawl in Beau's direction.

She didn't even make it a few feet before the vampire grabbed a fistful of her hair. She was pulled backwards, her butt hitting the pavement.

Still clutching her hair, the vampire began to drag her toward the car behind him.

Bradley grabbed his wrist, trying to pull herself free while her feet scrambled and kicked at the pavement. To her horror, she saw Beau take a two-by-four to the gut and double over.

The vampire fighting Beau loomed over him, his weapon raised for another blow.

That was the last thing Bradley saw before she was hauled from the ground and tossed into a trunk.

Deadly Encounters of the Supernatural Kind

Melissa Hosack

Whimsical Publications, LLC

Florida

Deadly Encounters of the Supernatural Kind is a work of fiction. Names, characters, and incidents are the products of the author's imagination and are either fictitious or are used fictitiously. Any resemblance to actual events or persons, living or dead, is entirely coincidental.

If you purchased this book without a cover, you should be aware that this book may have been stolen property and reported as "unsold and destroyed" to the publisher. In such case, neither the publisher nor the author has received payment for this "stripped book."

Published in the United States by
Whimsical Publications, LLC
Florida

http://www.whimsicalpublications.com

ISBN-13: 978-0-9787738-8-5

Printed in the United States of America

Prologue

Beauregard Channing stared at his best friend of four hundred years in stony silence.

Not fazed by Beau's attitude, Ashton Rutherford rushed on, "The artifact was found..." He rustled through some papers. "Ah! Here it is." He adjusted his glasses and squinted at his illegible handwriting. "It was found in Winston-Salem."

"Surprise there," Beau grumbled, rolling his eyes at the way Ashton cleaved to glasses he no longer needed.

Ashton looked up at him in surprise. "Beau, this is very important information. If this thing was to end up in the wrong hands..."

"I know. I know. Death and unspeakable evil," Beau said in a bored voice. He set Ashton with a thoughtful look. "You know, for a vampire, you have absolutely no fun."

Ashton looked aghast. "This isn't about having fun."

"Fine. I get it. We're all about not having fun. Just tell me who I'm hunting down this time. Gothic demon worshipper? A housewife with too much time on her hands? A faithful catholic just trying to do what's right?"

Ashton gave him an annoyed look, but said, "The item was recovered by a Bradley Hildebrand. Bradley moved the item to...somewhere in Bergen County, New Jersey. I don't have much more than that."

"Nothing like sending me in blind," Beau griped. Before Ashton could rush in with useless apologies, Beau said, "Bradley Hildebrand of Bergen County. Got it." He climbed to his feet, straightening to his full height of six feet two inches. "Mr. Hildebrand will be dead by the end of the week." He frowned. "At least he'd better be. I'm not missing kick off of the football season for this shit."

"This shit," Ashton chastised, "is the safety of humanity...and you don't have to kill..."

"Can't leave witnesses," Beau flippantly reminded him, waving off any protests. "It could mean the downfall of America."

"Very well then," Ashton conceded with a sigh. "You're the professional."

"That I am." As Beau strode to the door, he gave one last comment simply for the look of horror it would receive. "And for goodness sake, get out and eat someone. You look like death."

Chapter 1

Beau walked alone down the sidewalk of a college campus, taking in his surroundings with trepidation. If there was anything he hated more than sunlight, it was college students.

They were always so smug, so full of themselves. They thought just because they were furthering their education they knew everything there was to know about the world. What he wouldn't give to put them all in their places, perhaps rip out a few spines. He couldn't do that, though. Ashton would flip. Not that it was Ashton putting up with this crap.

Beau could hear the sound of music blaring through speakers. In the distance, he heard the screams and squeals of a party in full swing. A college campus on a Saturday night. What had he been thinking?

He knew exactly what he'd been thinking. It was easier to blend in with a crowd, easier to play human. Now all he had to do was track down Bradley, get the artifact, and snap the poor kid's neck. Easy. Clean. Done.

As he approached the packed lawn of a nearby fraternity house, Beau swept the area for prey. He looked for someone weak, someone easily manipulated that could lead him to this Bradley fellow. His eyes landed on a boy with shaggy blond hair.

The kid was off by himself, kicking around a ridiculous-looking bean pouch...a hacky sack, Beau recalled. He was far enough to the side that Beau could approach him without drawing anyone's attention. Besides, judging from the kid's appearance, he didn't exactly mesh with this preppy crowd.

Stepping up next to the scruffy-looking blond, Beau cleared his throat. "Excuse me," he said quietly, wanting to draw as little notice as possible.

The kid paused in his incessant kicking, his foot frozen in the air with the ball still on it. "Yo," he replied with a bob of his head in greeting.

Beau fought not to roll his eyes. "I am looking for a Bradley Hildebrand. You wouldn't happen to know...?" He trailed off, a question in his voice.

The kid broke into a giant grin. "I know Bradley." Grabbing the hacky sack and shoving it deep into his pocket, the kid stuck out his chest boastfully. "You came to the right guy because I am none other than Bradley's best friend. Have been since the two of us were wearing diapers."

"Of course you are," Beau said dryly. "Lucky me." His sarcasm was lost on the kid in front of him.

"I'm Camden," the kid introduced, offering a hand.

Beau stared at the hand for a moment, then asked in a bored tone, "Where is Bradley?"

"Bradley," Camden said with a snap of his fingers, "right." He nodded toward the building behind him. "Follow me." With that, Camden raced off.

Trying to keep a look of aggravation off his face, Beau followed at a much more dignified pace. He'd let the kid run off some energy. "If Bradley is anything like you," Beau grumbled, "I'll be doing the world a favor by snapping his scrawny little neck."

He entered the fraternity house and took a look around him in disgust. In almost every hand was an alcoholic beverage or a cigarette. In the far corner, he caught the scent of marijuana coming from two girls who barely looked eighteen. Next to the girls, a couple was pressed up against the wall, not seeming to care about the fact that they were mating in public. Sometimes it was hard to remember why he was watching out for their welfare. Oh, right. It was because Ashton made him. Beau's lip tugged at the corner at that thought and he almost smiled. Almost.

A redhead in a skimpy halter top and mini skirt pulled him away from all thoughts of Ashton as she grabbed onto his arm. "I haven't seen you in any of my classes," she breathed.

The sour smell of alcohol wafted into Beau's face, and his lip curled in distaste as he glanced down at the cleavage she was pressing into his arm. "I wasn't aware prostitution had become a major."

Before the girl's intoxicated brain could comprehend the insult, he wrapped an arm around her waist and hauled her up against his chest. Putting his mouth next to her ear, he whispered, "Relax."

Her body went limp in his arms, her breath coming from between her lips in a soft whisper. Her eyes, already unfocused from her drinking, became blank, lifeless.

Brushing her hair away from her neck, Beau leaned down and let his fangs sink into her throat. He took slow, measured gulps, making sure that, to any witness, it would look like nothing more than an embrace from a lover.

The girl tasted bitter, like stale beer and vodka.

Though he could have used the blood for extra strength, Beau pulled back after only a few mouthfuls. If Bradley's friend was any indication, Beau would be just fine in the muscle department. He gave the girl's neck a quick lick of his tongue, hiding any evidence of his invasion.

Releasing her waist, he pulled back, staring down into her glassy green eyes with his dark blue ones. "You are drunk, darling. I would suggest you go home." He went to leave and her grip tightened on his arm, her nails digging into his skin.

"Don't go," she begged. She licked her lips eagerly, the invitation coming easier than it should for any respectable woman. "Come home with me."

Beau let out a weary sigh. Drinking from mortals often left them aroused. The feeding was something primal and sexual to their subconscious minds. It was an unfamiliar experience, but instinctual habit took over, telling their bodies to find pleasure in the act. To them it was pure ecstasy.

It had stopped being that way for him a long time ago. Now, it was merely a tool of survival. There was no thrill to it anymore. It was more of a hassle than anything else. Reaching out, Beau grabbed the closest male and yanked him over by the collar. "Deal with this," he ordered, shoving the redhead into the person's arms.

Lucky for him, the redhead was easily distracted. She went willingly into the new man's arms, her mouth on his before the guy could even realize what was happening.

That was another reason feeding had lost its thrill. To the mortals, it wasn't about him. It was about his power and what he could do, what he represented. He, as a man, was forgotten moments after such intimate encounters. He'd grown tired of pretending the interactions were anything more than meaningless stimulation and a means of continuing his existence.

With a revolted look, Beau left them locked in their embrace, his eyes sweeping the room for Camden. It didn't take him long to spot the shaggy-haired blond. It wasn't like the poor kid blended well. "Camden," he growled out between clenched teeth.

Camden whirled around, and then had to shake his hair out of his eyes. "Dude!" he called out. "I just found Bradley!" He spun back to the person he was speaking to, his lanky body completely overshadowing the other person. "Bradley," he practically hollered, "this guy here's been looking for you."

Beau stepped forward to stand next to Camden and his words died in his throat.

Standing before him was a girl with loose, black curls cascading halfway down her back and the most startling blue eyes he'd ever seen. She looked around five foot nine, tall for a girl, but still tiny and fragile when standing next to him.

She was dressed differently than the rest of the women here; less trashy were the only words that came to his mind. She was wearing a dark blue sundress that really brought out the color in her eyes. Her feet were adorned in strappy, black heels.

It was so cute, so arousing, that he wanted to shove her against the wall and... Beau shook his head to clear those thoughts from his mind. Contemplations like those were not something he was used to. They were things he hadn't thought of in a very long time. He was startled by his initial attraction to the girl in front of him. What was it about her that piqued his interest after all this time? Pushing that to the back of his mind, he concentrated on the important details. "You're not Bradley," he denied stubbornly. It was impossible for this girl to be the person he'd been sent here to murder. Besides being too beautiful, she was too...female.

She blinked at him in surprise. "Yes, I am," she said with a giggle.

"You're a girl," Beau needlessly pointed out, looking for any reason to deny that she was the one he was hunting down. He frowned at the sound of her laughter, finding it distracting.

She smiled, showing off the brightest teeth he'd ever seen. "Yes. A girl named Bradley." She crossed her arms under her chest, drawing his gaze to her breasts, and eyed him questioningly. "And you are?"

"This is," Camden began, but trailed off when he realized Beau had never given his name. "Yeah! Who are you?"

Clearing his throat, Beau drew his eyes back to her face. "I am Beauregard Channing, but you can just call me Beau." He'd spoken before his brain could stop him. He'd never given out his real name to a target before.

A target? Is that what she was? A target? Somehow, snapping Bradley's neck didn't sound as fun as it had half an hour ago.

"All right...Beau," she said, narrowing her eyes playfully. "You were looking for me...?" She trailed off, a question in her voice.

Beau had to swallow, unable to get his vocal cords to cooperate. "I was wondering if we could speak in private."

Bradley's eyes slid to Camden, and she sent him a slightly concerned look that said she wasn't sure if she should trust Beau enough to go off alone with him.

Good girl, Beau silently praised her. He'd seen too many girls her age go willingly with a stranger. He'd never once had a problem finding blood donors to follow him into dark alleys. People were too trusting. Seeing as he was one of the dangers lurking in the night, he knew first hand...not that he had any plans of making Bradley a midnight snack. The thought of hurting her was something he wished to avoid at all cost. Just this once, perhaps, he could leave a witness behind.

Bradley's blue gaze shifted back to him. "What did you want to speak with me about?"

Beau's cool eyes traveled over her face, attempting to look bored. "A colleague of mine..." His eyes began searching the people closest to them. He didn't trust the others in the crowded room. They didn't look like a threat, but he'd learned in the past that people often hid dark intentions behind faux ignorance.

He stepped closer to her, lowering his voice to a whisper. "I have a colleague that is interested in a piece of jewelry you recently procured." He arched an eyebrow. "An interesting piece of jewelry with Pagan origin."

"My grandmother's necklace?" she asked in surprise. Her blue eyes searched his face in uncertainty. "I figured the symbols had meaning, but Pagan?" She shook her head vehemently. "I don't think so."

Beau's lip quirked and he forced back a grin. This girl had no clue as to how powerful of an item she had in her possession. Apparently, Granny had kept a few secrets. Trying to stay patient, Beau said, "My colleague wishes to purchase your Pagan artifact."

Bradley shook her head. "No," she said, voice firm with resolve . "It was my grandmother's. I don't want to sell it." Her eyes narrowed in suspicion. "How do you know about it anyway? The only person who knew about it was that historian..." Those beautiful blue eyes darkened. "Is your colleague that insistent Ashton fellow I spoke to online?"

Beau rolled his eyes and fought back a groan. What was Ashton thinking giving out his real name? And a historian? Only because he'd lived it. Beau's next statement caught even himself off guard. "Perhaps you would allow me to take you out to dinner tomorrow evening. I could at least get a look at your necklace and assess its authenticity."

In all his years, Beau had never offered to pay for a piece Ashton was hunting, let alone ask the owner to dinner. He'd normally be standing over a body at this point, taking whatever it was he wanted.

"You're asking me out?" Bradley asked, eyes widening in surprise.

He could hear her pulse quicken, could see the slight flush of her skin. Her body language stated just how appealing she found his suggestion.

A cocky smirk touched Beau's lips as he leaned closer to her, twirling a dark lock of her hair around his finger. "I was sent here to retrieve that necklace," he breathed in her ear. "The means of negotiation are open, and any illicit acts that happen to occur simply sweeten our business interaction."

He felt her shiver. Ever so gently, he ran his fingertips over her bare arms, caressing the Goosebumps that had sprung up at his offer. Perhaps this trip would be beneficial to him, unlike most of the missions Ashton sent him on.

Bradley's hand was suddenly on his chest, pushing him backwards and putting distance between the two of them. "There isn't going to be any negotiation. I'm not giving you the necklace."

Her eyes traveled over his body, lingering on his broad chest. Her breath hitched in her throat for a second before she grumbled, "And as for your other request, I will have to decline. You should be ashamed of yourself, offering sex as payment for..." She shook her head, her expression one of disapproval.

"The sex doesn't have to be payment. It can just be sex."

Bradley sucked in an audible gasp. It took her a moment to compose herself, but she finally managed to say, "I'm sorry, but..." She seemed to struggle with her answer. "No, Mr. Channing." As if trying to keep him from noticing the blush on her cheeks, she chastised, "I don't believe your offers are appropriate, or very professional."

"Some things are more desirable than professionalism." He watched with hidden glee as she struggled to compose herself, fighting back the urge to accept his oh so tempting offers.

"I'm sorry, Mr. Channing, but the answer is no. Please tell your colleague that I do not wish to be bothered with any more...insulting offers." She gave him a pointed look, once again crossing her arms under her chest. "If you don't mind..."

Beau's eyebrows shot up in surprise. She was asking him to leave. She was turning down his offer. Could she *do* that? He couldn't remember the last time he'd been so carelessly dismissed.

His eyes drifted, once again, to her crossed arms, more importantly her breasts, but he used her arms as an alibi. "Such a hostile disposition. Your body language, your posture, that unhappy pout on your face, all suggest that you do not find me amusing in the least."

She arched one delicate eyebrow as if to say, *Duh.*

Beau's eyes narrowed at her. If only she knew his original intention had been to snap that pretty little neck. Maybe then she wouldn't be so quick to turn her nose up at his adjustment to the plan.

"Fine," Beau said with a sneer. As he turned on his heels to leave, he grabbed the front of Camden's shirt and yanked the blond roughly after him.

Chapter 2

Bradley watched Beau drag Camden away and almost followed after them to give the infuriating stranger a piece of her mind. Just who did he think he was? He had no right to put his hands on Camden. Her eyes narrowing, she glared in the direction they had gone.

Beau had Camden backed into a corner and was speaking with a dark, angry look on his face. If he thought he was going to get to her through Camden, he was crazy.

Camden wasn't going to convince her to change her mind, nor would he even try. There was also no way she'd ever trade a family heirloom for sex. Sure, Beau was good-looking with that thick, shoulder length, black hair and his captivating blue eyes, but he wasn't *that* good-looking.

"There you are," a voice grumbled behind her.

Glad for the distraction, Bradley dragged her eyes from Beau's muscled arms to stare at her ex-boyfriend, Carter. She stayed silent, her eyes icy.

"I've been looking all over for you," he complained.

"And I've been standing around this juvenile party twiddling my thumbs, waiting for you." She gave him an impatient look before adding, "What was so important that it couldn't wait?"

Carter puffed his chest out in an attempt to look important. "My things," he demanded. "I left a few of my possessions in your room and I will be needing them back."

Bradley's eyebrows arched in disbelief. "You couldn't just stop by and pick them up?"

Carter shifted his weight and avoided looking directly at her. "I was afraid you'd make a big deal about it and get all weepy. You know how I hate that."

"When have you ever seen me get weepy?" she asked in

annoyance.

He gave Bradley a sympathetic look that said he didn't believe her, but honored her bravery. "I didn't want you to get all clingy on me and beg me to take you back. I've moved on. I think you should too." He gave her a pointed look before continuing with, "I figured you would be less likely to make a scene in a crowd."

"Oh, for heaven's sake!" Bradley cried, throwing her hands up. "Remind me again why I ever went out with you."

"I often ask myself the same thing," Carter mumbled, slightly disgruntled.

At that moment, Kristie Taylor walked up and put a tentative hand on Carter's arm. "She's not making a scene is she? I thought you said she wouldn't make a scene."

"Unbelievable," Bradley griped.

Carter put an arm around the buxom blonde's shoulder. "I needed a woman with passion," he informed Bradley. "Someone not afraid to express herself."

Bradley knew that Carter was a creep, but the words stung all the same. It was never fun to have an ex insult your relationship skills. "Maybe I wasn't very passionate with you because you kiss like a fish," she snapped back. "You're all rubber lips and drool. I wanted to wear a bib to keep my clothes clean."

Kristie's gray eyes widened in alarm, and she shot a glance at Carter.

"Also," Bradley added, feeling as if she was on a roll, and delighted at the horrified look on Carter's face. "The guy I'm with now has not a single complaint. We've got passion out the wazoo!" She waved a hand in the air, her mouth continuing on without her brain. "So, if you want your things, dredge up a little bit of nerve and come get them. Now, if you'll excuse me, I have to get back to a man who is more than talented at kissing."

With a superior huff, she spun on her heels and marched toward the corner where Camden and Beau were still talking heatedly...well, at least Beau was. Camden was just listening with wide, green eyes.

Instantly regretting letting her motor mouth run wild, Bradley grabbed Beau's arm. The minute he turned to look at her, she pressed herself against his chest and stood on tiptoes to brush her lips against his.

His initial reaction was shock, but that was quickly replaced with desire. Taking the opportunity before she changed her mind, Beau deepened the kiss.

Bradley gave a surprised gasp into his mouth when one of his arms wrapped around her waist and hauled her up against his chest.

He buried his other hand in her hair while his mouth molded to hers. He nipped and teased at her lips, his fingers caressing along her back.

Caught by surprise at the fervor of their kiss, Bradley let out a soft whimper and gripped at the sleeves of his royal blue dress shirt.

After a moment, Beau pulled back and looked down at her with a playful, questioning expression on his face. "Not that I'm complaining, but what was that for?"

Bradley couldn't find the breath to answer him. She'd never been kissed like that in her life. Nothing even came close. With a frown, she contemplated the fact that it had been with this insultingly arrogant man. Her frown deepened as she glanced over her shoulder to look at Carter.

He was staring at her in open-mouthed surprise, his jaw practically at his feet.

"Ex-boyfriend," Camden, the traitor, informed Beau. "He's been giving her a lot of crap."

Beau's lips curved into a devilish grin. "So you're trying to exact some revenge in the form of me?" His eyes slid to Carter. "What's to stop me from causing a scene and yelling about the crazy lady who just sexually harassed me?"

Camden snickered, but Bradley found nothing funny in that statement. "Please don't humiliate me," she begged, hating the desperation in her voice.

"What is it worth to you?" Beau asked coyly.

"What?" she cried in disbelief. "You're blackmailing me?" She wouldn't have been able to keep the indignant squeak from her voice even if she tried.

Beau nodded with a smug grin. "I most certainly am. You have dinner with me tomorrow night to discuss your heirloom. If you do this, I will help make that ex-boyfriend of yours jealous." It wasn't exactly the most conventional trade, but he needed to get that necklace.

"I don't care if he's jealous or not," Bradley snapped in agitation. "I honestly don't. It's just that he..." She broke off, a faint blush touching her cheeks. "Well...he said that..." Sounding as if she feared it was true, she finished, "He said I didn't have any passion."

Beau surveyed Carter in distaste. "You did not seem passionless to me," he commented. Looking down into her eyes, he added, "Though another sample may be needed to correctly assess the situation."

"Oh, no!" she cried, putting a hand to his chest to stop his advances. "Not again. Just keep your lips to yourself, buddy. This is a kiss free zone."

He gave her a lopsided grin that she hated to admit caused butterflies to flutter around in her stomach. "So are we on for dinner, darling?" The word *darling* dripped with sarcasm.

She let out a weary sigh and ran a hand over her face. "If I agree, will you go away and leave me alone after this ridiculous dinner in which I will, once again, refuse any offers you make?"

Beau slid an arm around her shoulders. "And which offers would you be referring to? The sexual offers, or the ones to acquire your artifact?"

She elbowed him in the stomach, but he didn't seem to notice. "I will turn down *any* offers," she assured.

He gave a noncommittal shrug. "We shall see."

She rolled her eyes with a huff. "You are absolutely impossible."

He gave an exaggerated wink. "Yeah, but you love me anyway." His grin widened, taking on an almost mocking curve at the corners. "You can't resist the passion I bring out in you." He paused, his eyes lowering seductively to her mouth. "You are an absolutely fantastic kisser, by the way."

Bradley rolled her eyes again, having a feeling he wasn't going to be deterred as easily as she'd hoped.

Chapter 3

Bradley stormed into the small, dimly lit diner just off campus. She was dripping wet with her hair plastered to her face from the pounding rain. She was shivering cold and grumpy. Part of her poor attitude was from being dragged out this late. Last night, she'd begged Beau to meet her for lunch instead of dinner because she had a night class from six to nine.

He'd refused, insisting on dinner.

By the time Bradley got home from her class, changed, and walked in the pouring rain all the way to the diner they'd agreed to meet at, it was after ten-thirty. Her eyes narrowed as she caught sight of Beau in the back corner.

He looked cozy and dry...and perhaps even better looking than the night before. He wore a dark green dress shirt with the sleeves rolled up, showing off a pair of muscled forearms. The deep shade of green looked absolutely gorgeous with his hair.

His dry hair, Bradley silently reminded herself just for a reason to be annoyed at him, and to help her forget how he made her weak in the knees. Just because he was cute didn't change the fact that he was irritating and in no way likable.

"Even soaking wet you look adorable," Beau said in approval as she approached the table.

She made sure to give him a glowering look to show just how unimpressed she was with his comment. Sliding out of her powder blue raincoat, she shook it out, taking small satisfaction when water droplets splashed the front of Beau's shirt.

"You've got the matching raincoat and hat," he continued, not in the least bit deterred. His eyes ventured to her feet. "And powder blue, knee high rubber boots," he practically cooed. "That is too cute."

"Bite me," Bradley snapped, sliding into the seat across from him. She might have been tempted to take delight in his compliment, but she knew he didn't really mean it. There was a slight mocking, sarcastic tone to his voice that wasn't there quite enough for her to call him on it. It was as if he was making fun of her, but halfheartedly.

She ripped the hat from her head and tossed it to the bench next to her. She knew her hair must look horrific. She could feel that it was limp and dripping rain.

Beau arched an eyebrow and handed her a menu. "Apparently you're one of those people who get grouchy when they're hungry."

She snatched the menu from his fingers and began perusing its contents. "No, I'm one of those people that don't like to be cold or wet...or eat after ten, or have half a bottle of bleach dumped on me."

Beau blinked back his surprise. "I'm fairly certain the bleach incident wasn't my fault."

"No," she agreed huffily. "We were in the lab tonight and Camden dumped bleach all over the front of me. Do you know how badly the fumes burn your eyes when your clothes practically take a bath in bleach?"

"Can't say that I do," Beau said in amusement. His eyes squinted at her in suspicion. "Why were you playing with bleach anyway? What kind of class is this?"

"Chemistry."

His eyebrows rose, a habit Bradley was finding quite adorable. She shook her head, trying to clear herself of that thought. It wasn't adorable. It was annoying.

"What are they teaching you to do, build a bomb?"

"No," Bradley cried, appalled. She went to comment further, but the waitress appeared at their table and asked for their orders.

Scanning the menu one last time, Bradley said, "I'll just take a burger and fries...ooh and a bowl of chicken noodle soup." She sent Beau a glare as if daring him to comment. "And perhaps an appetizer of mozzarella sticks to start off with...and a hot chocolate."

The waitress reached to grab her menu and Bradley gave it one last, quick look. "And a coke." Feeling a need to explain herself, she added, "That way I have something to drink while the hot chocolate is cooling down."

The waitress stared at Bradley for a moment, then shrugged and started writing the order down. "Sure thing, honey," she drawled, snapping her gum. Her eyes lifted to Beau. "What'll you have?"

Beau gave her a brilliant, charming smile. "I'll have what the delicate little lady is having."

Bradley kicked him in the shin.

His smile turned into a grimace for half a second before returning full force.

As the waitress turned and walked away, Bradley hissed, "You're a sleezeball."

Beau's face took on a look of surprised innocence.

"Oh, don't pull that crap! You didn't hear me telling the waitress that I'd have the same thing the ogre across from me chooses."

Beau's eyes twinkled in delight. "Well, this ogre didn't even get a chance to say what he wanted before you ordered half the menu."

"Half the menu?" Bradley squeaked. "For your information, if you would have met me for lunch, I would have eaten dinner *before* I went to class. It's your fault I'm so hungry."

"Lunch was undoable," he said dismissively.

"And further more," she pressed on, "maybe I wouldn't have had to order the soup if I wasn't freezing. Also, your fault."

Beau's lip quirked. "Perhaps you could have chosen to come sit over here and let *me* warm you up."

Bradley's eyes narrowed, but she bit back her nasty retort when the waitress reappeared with the mozzarella sticks and two bowls of soup.

The waitress ignored Bradley's dirty look just as easily as Beau did. Without even a questioning glance, she sauntered away.

As soon as the waitress was out of hearing range, Beau rushed forward to speak before Bradley could. "I am honestly sorry that I have caused you such hunger. It was not my intent. Had it been at all possible, I would have met you for lunch."

"Anything's possible," was Bradley's grumbled reply.

"Trust me, my dear," Beau said, grinning with some personal amusement, "meeting you for lunch was quite impossible." His foot rubbed against hers underneath the table. "Now," he said, drawing out the word, "would you like me to warm away any thoughts of that chilly rain?"

Bradley ignored the excited pitter-patter her heart gave and slid her foot away from his. "No," she said darkly.

"Very well," Beau said with a weary sigh. "On to business then, I suppose." His eyes slid to her purse, and he held out a hand. "Can I see the artifact?"

She squirmed in her seat. "I didn't bring it." She avoided eye contact by spooning some soup into her mouth.

Beau dropped his silverware in surprise at her statement. She heard it clatter to the table and could only imagine the look she was receiving.

"You didn't bring it?!" Beau hissed. "That's the entire reason we're here tonight. Why in the world wouldn't you bring it?"

Bradley finally looked up, speaking in her own defense. "How was I to know you weren't some crazy lunatic that was going to bludgeon me over the head and take my grandma's necklace? You said you wanted to *discuss* it, so talk, pal."

"I do believe you are purposely being difficult," Beau accused, "but whatever. We'll just talk."

Bradley nodded her approval. "Good," she said, breaking a mozzarella stick into four pieces and nibbling on one of the tiny bits. "Me first." She set him with a suspicious look. "Why do you want my grandmother's necklace so badly? You guys are far too persistent to just be collectors." Her eyes roamed over his broad chest, his muscled arms. "And you don't look like a historian."

Beau's expression turned smug at her last comment. It was quickly replaced by a look of trepidation. "I don't think you'd be very accepting of the truth," he said, voice hesitant.

"If you don't tell me the truth," she snapped in reply, "I will never let you near me again and you can just kiss seeing that necklace goodbye."

"Fine," Beau came back in an almost challenging tone. "You want the truth, you got it." He paused dramatically. "I'm a vampire." He didn't get to say anything else because the waitress reappeared.

While she went about setting out their food, Bradley just stared at Beau from across the table. As soon as the waitress was out of hearing range, Bradley hissed, "You're what?"

"A vampire," Beau said calmly. He himself was surprised at how easy it was for him to admit that. Never before in his four hundred years had he told a mortal what he was. It was stupid. It was careless. It was a good way to find yourself on the receiving end of a stake.

There was just something about Bradley, though, that made him want to confide in her. He was trusting a hit with information on how to kill him. Crazy. Stupid. But refreshing.

On her disbelieving look, Beau said, "I told you that you wouldn't like the truth, but it does help explain why I couldn't make lunch."

Bradley took a big bite of her burger and glared at him from across the table. Around her food, she said, "Of all the bullshit lies I've ever heard, this is the absolute worst." She gave a casual shrug. "However, I give you bonus points for creativity." She sounded calm and collected, not at all perturbed by his revelation.

It ruffled his feathers a bit that she wasn't cowering in her seat, trying not to scream in terror. "I am telling the truth," Beau came back unhappily. "That necklace is a Wiccan talisman with more power than you could ever imagine. In the wrong hands, it could be devastating. Every dark witch and wizard has been searching for that thing for the past fifty years, and now it shows up in your possession." Beau set her with a serious look. "Others would not be as gentle to you as I have been. I think you should take that into consideration."

Bradley drummed her fingers on the table, giving away her nervousness. "What do you intend to do with it?" she asked in anxiety. "Do you have dark plans, as well?"

"I'm a vampire," Beau gently reminded her. "I'm not going to gain any power from such an item. I merely hope to put it into hiding so that it doesn't get into the wrong hands."

"So you're looking out for us poor humans. Is that it? You're a humanitarian."

"Hardly," he grumbled back. "Ashton is the one with the big, human loving heart. I'm in it merely for the violence. Normally, after making the owner of such items suffer unspeakable torture, I'd have them begging me to take whatever it is I want." He paused, letting that sink in. "Then, I'd snap their neck."

Bradley's eyes widened in horror, realizing she was one

of those people.

"Oh, don't worry," Beau reassured. "I find you far too adorable to torture."

"Thanks?" she said uncertainly. Wanting to get away from the torture subject, she asked, "How come a talisman won't work for a vampire?"

"I shouldn't even be telling you this..." Beau glanced around them as if expecting the vampire police to jump out at any second. Finally, when he was certain no one was listening to them, he said, "Vampires can't do magic. We can't cast spells or do charms. All of us are born with certain skills or powers. You can add all the witchy artifacts you want, but we're not going to learn the skill hidden within the object. It's either in our hardwiring or it isn't."

He paused, taking a bite of one of his fries. "Most witches are born with some magic of their own, but most of it is taught. Much of it needs certain items, like your necklace, to work at full potential."

"Okay," Bradley said, drawing out the word, "I'll bite. What exactly is it that my necklace can do?"

"Raise the dead," Beau said casually, taking a bite of his burger.

"Raise the dead?" Bradley squeaked in horror. She didn't buy into his whole fantasy world, but still, the thought of having something sitting in her bedroom that could possibly raise the dead was spooky. "You mean like a zombie?"

"Not like a zombie," Beau corrected. "Like a person. You can bring the deceased back to the state they were in before their death. There were a lot of really bad people taken out before they got a big enough following to do severe damage. To bring them back with a second shot at their campaign of death and violence would be devastating." He waved a hand as if trying to explain. "The paranormal world has been on shaky ground recently. There have been a ton of dark entities popping up. Too many could tip the balance between good and evil."

"That would be bad."

"Yes," Beau said with a mocking grin. "Dark entities tend to be bad."

"You aren't a dark entity?" Bradley asked, uncertain of where his allegiance was.

Beau glared and took another bite of his burger. "Do I

look like a hell spawn?"

Bradley thought he looked like anything but a hell spawn. Hell spawns didn't have a body to drool over. A hell spawn's muscles didn't ripple with every movement. She had to blink to pull herself together. Getting herself under control, she said in her defense, "You said you'd planned on snapping my neck. That sounds pretty evil, if you ask me."

"I didn't do it, though," he argued, as if that made it okay. "Trust me. If I were evil, we would not be on a date right now. You would be lying face down in an alley somewhere."

"Date?" she squeaked, finding this more disturbing than the alley comment. "You think this is a date?"

He gave a casual shrug. "We're eating an intimate dinner together. I fully intend to pay for your meal, and you dressed up in those sexy boots for me."

She glanced under the table at her rubber rain boots and gave him a funny look.

"Also," Beau continued, "I have every intention of seducing you once we're through with dinner. That sounds like a date to me."

Bradley gave a squawk of protest. "What did I tell you? We've already been over this. There will be no kissing and absolutely no seducing."

"If you remember, you seduced me first, so I get a freebie," he reasoned. "It's only fair."

"Well, that...that's illogical," she stammered.

Beau shrugged and took another bite of his burger.

Grasping at something to change the subject, Bradley accused, "You're eating!"

He paused in mid-chew, eyeing her in puzzlement. "Yeah. And?"

"You said you were a vampire. This proves that you obviously aren't. Vampires don't eat burgers. That means you *aren't* a vampire. So there!"

Beau resumed his chewing, not looking too fazed by her declaration. "Don't believe everything you hear." He gave a sigh and set her with those captivating blue eyes. "You're really putting stress on this relationship by believing every rumor you hear about my kind."

"Rumor?" Bradley rolled her eyes. "Vampires don't exist to have untrue rumors spreading around about them. They are fictional characters...and you," she said, popping her last fry into her mouth, "have run out of time." She picked up her purse. "You have not convinced me to give up my necklace. You have not convinced me that you are a vampire. You have not convinced me of anything. Thank you very much for dinner and the...unique company, but I really must be going."

Beau stood when she did, snatching up her coat before she could stop him. "I'll walk you home." He held her coat up so she could slip into it.

She hesitated, but finally let him help her into the coat. "That's unnecessary."

"I insist," came his reply, his fingers grazing lightly along her throat as he adjusted her collar.

She shivered at the sensation of his fingertips against her skin, but played it off as a chill from thinking about the cold she would soon be facing. She pulled her jacket around herself for warmth, not that a rubber raincoat gave much, and then bent down to adjust her boots. She fiddled with her hat, making sure it was securely on her head in preparation of heading out into the rain.

She let out a little huff. Oh, who was she kidding? She was stalling in hopes that he'd stick to his offer of paying for her dinner and walking her home. She frowned. *No, I don't think this is a date,* she silently chided herself in sarcasm.

She watched him remove his wallet from his back pocket, completely riveted by his smooth, graceful movements. He was like poetry.

Their dinner didn't cost more than forty dollars, even with the tip, but he pulled out a hundred dollar bill and dropped it to the table.

"A bit much, don't you think?" she asked a little scornfully.

Beau smiled. "When you've been around as long as I have, you store up a decent amount of money." His grin widened. "Besides, I'm trying to impress my date."

"This is not a date," Bradley reminded him as they made their way to the door. When they reached it, she gave a huff of annoyance as Beau held it open for her. Rolling her eyes, she marched through, not even glancing in his direction. Without a word, she began marching toward her apartment at a brisk pace.

"It's pouring," Beau observed, stating the obvious. "Wouldn't you rather take a cab?"

Bradley stopped in her tracks and spun back around to face him. "No," she answered haughtily. "For those of us poor college students who aren't oozing with money, we like to save our cash for something worthwhile." She sent him a sideways glance. "Are vampires like witches?" she asked in mockery. "Are you afraid you'll melt?"

With an exaggerated roll of his eyes, Beau stepped out into the downpour. "You've seen the *Wizard of Oz* one too many times. Witches don't melt. If they did, you'd be in an awful lot of trouble right now with all this rain."

Bradley gave an indignant gasp and screeched to a halt. She turned to give him an angered look. "Well, look who's changed his tune. What happened to Mr. This Is A Date?"

A martyred look crossed his face. "Easy, killer. Relax. It was not a jab at your shining personality." He did an air quote, and there was a sarcastic emphasis on the word *shining*. "That last statement *was* a jab, by the way," he felt the need to add. "You inherited an item of witchcraft. I'm guessing that's not the only thing your grandmother passed on to you."

"My grandmother was not a witch!" Bradley cried with a stamp of her foot.

"I bet she was, just like I'm betting you are. Witchcraft is also the only explanation as to why I haven't killed you yet. You've put some kind of charm on me to make me desire you."

"Oh, I have not!" Bradley griped, resuming her trek through the downpour. "Besides, witches don't exist."

"Just like vampires don't exist?" he came back almost smugly with a wave at his chest, as if he were the living proof of a contradiction.

"You are not a vampire," she informed him, sounding exasperated.

He sent her a sideways glance. "You have no idea how temping it is to tear your throat out with my fangs to prove my point."

She narrowed her eyes, but suggested, "Why don't you turn into a bat? That oughtta prove it."

"We don't turn into bats," he came back in disgust.

"So, you don't turn into bats and you eat burgers.

Sounds like the real deal to me," she taunted sarcastically.

"I *am* the real deal," Beau growled in agitation.

"Prove it," she challenged. "Show me some fang."

With an aggravated sigh, he stopped, pulling her to a halt next to him. "Fine." He bared his teeth and his face screwed up in concentration. "I don't really do this unless I'm feeding," he said in obvious annoyance at the inconvenience of her request.

Bradley braced her hands on his forearms and stood on tiptoes so she could peer into his mouth. "I don't see anything."

Confusion flitted across his features. "I don't understand..." He concentrated with all his might, but couldn't seem to get his fangs to spring forward.

"They shy?" Bradley teased. Slapping him on the chest, she stepped back. "See? No proof. Not a vampire." With a little sigh, she started walking again. "Why do all the really sexy ones have to be crazy?"

Beau followed her, rubbing a finger along his teeth and gums, perplexed. "I just don't get it. This never..." He trailed off with a grin. "You said I was sexy."

"I also said you were crazy," she pointed out as they reached her building. Glancing over her shoulder at the door, she said, "Well, this is me."

When she spun back around, Beau stood with his hands in his pockets, his thumbs sticking out in a very rugged and manly way. She had to mentally count to ten to keep herself from ogling him. "Goodnight," she said through clenched teeth.

"I suppose I'll be seeing you soon," he said. "We've still got unfinished business to discuss."

"Not really. I'm not giving your vampire wannabe butt my necklace, so that pretty much deters me from having any further interaction with you."

"Oh, there will be plenty more interaction."

Bradley couldn't help but notice that the low, husky sound of his voice sent tingles along her skin, affecting her like no one ever had before.

She studied the way little water droplets glistened on the ends of his shoulder length, jet-black hair. Her eyes skimmed over his broad chest, hungrily taking in the way his shirt clung to every muscle.

She was so busy admiring his physique that she didn't notice he was going to kiss her until it was too late. Before she could even think about stopping him, Beau's lips were on hers.

They caressed across hers, soft and tentative as his arm snaked around her waist. He pulled her gently toward him until her body melded against his.

As if they had a mind of their own, Bradley's arms wrapped around his waist, clutching the back of his shirt in her fists.

His mouth became more persistent against hers, nudging her lips apart.

Pressing her body to his, she mumbled into his mouth, "This means nothing."

He nibbled at her bottom lip, drawing a gasp from her.

"This is just..." She tightened her fists, nails raking briefly against his skin. "This is just that freebie. You know that, right?"

Beau hissed at the sensation of her nails, his free hand rising to bury itself in her hair, gently gripping it at the scalp. "Then I'll use it wisely," he growled into her mouth.

"I still think," she said between kisses, "that you are arrogant, delusional, and should really see a psychologist about this vampire-" She broke off with a surprised yip as he pulled her more forcefully against his chest.

"Shut up," he grumbled, pausing only briefly before crushing his lips to hers again.

Bradley relaxed against him, making a happy mewing noise when he caressed her cheek with the back of his hand. She was just starting to fully enjoy herself when a sharp pain invaded her lower lip. An instant later, she tasted blood.

Beau moaned, drawing her lip into his mouth, sucking at her bleeding flesh.

She let out a squeak of protest and pushed her hands against his chest, shoving roughly as she tore her mouth from his.

His eyes were dilated, the irises darker than usual. He had a set of sharp fangs protruding from his mouth with her blood clinging to them, and his breathing was coming in shallow gasps.

She could see blood lust in his eyes almost as plain as his desire. She backed up a step in horror as his tongue flicked over his bloody teeth.

"Bradley," he practically begged as she took another step back, "I tried to warn you."

When he reached a hand out to her, she gave a cry of terror. "Stay away from me!" she shrieked before turning and racing into the building. As she shut the door behind her, she prayed that she was shutting Beauregard Channing out of her life indefinitely.

Chapter 4

Beau didn't even pause at Camden's surprised look as he pushed into the kid's dorm room. "You're going to help me." It was nearing dawn, early, but Beau had more important things on his mind than the kid's sleep. Besides, if Camden didn't want company, he shouldn't open the door to a relative stranger.

Camden blinked at the now empty hallway of the males only dormitory for a moment, startled that Beau had just shoved his way in as soon as the door was cracked open. His sleep filled eyes full of confusion, Camden shut the door and turned to face Beau. "What exactly are you asking for my help with?"

"I'm not asking," Beau stated, surveying the cramped room in distaste. He spun to give Camden a narrow-eyed look. "You got a roommate?"

The look on Camden's face let Beau know that the kid found his question off the wall, but he answered anyway. "Technically, yes, but I haven't seen him in over two months. His girlfriend has an off-campus apartment, and he moved in with her."

"Good. I need somewhere to hide out for the day."

Camden's eyebrows rose. "Hide out? What are you, a felon?" A thought seemed to occur to him. "And who said you could stay here?"

Beau rolled his eyes as he sunk down onto a beat up couch. "If that's the story you want to go with, sure. I'm a felon...and don't act like I'll bother you much. You told me the other night that you have classes all day Monday. You won't even be here."

"When?" Camden asked indignantly. "When you had me backed up in the corner threatening my life because Bradley gave you the cold shoulder?"

Beau gave him a warning glare, but forced his face to look as friendly as possible. "Regardless of the circumstances, you still said it."

"True," Camden said slowly, giving in to Beau's reasoning.

"Now," Beau said, seeing the issue of his lodging settled, "I need you to help me get in touch with Bradley. Something non-threatening so she can relax and just listen to what I have to say instead of freaking out."

"Freaking out?" Camden asked in confusion. "Why would she freak out?"

"Because she's afraid of me," Beau stated.

"Why? She find out you were a felon?" Camden's eyes widened at that thought. "A felon is in love with my best friend."

Beau's eyes widened in alarm. "First off, I am not in love with Bradley," he said firmly.

Before he could say anything further, Camden cut him off. "You're not going to go serial killer and chop her to bits are you?"

Beau's eyebrows furrowed. "Why would I do that?" He shook his head in disbelief, trying not to linger on the thought of how mentally unbalanced Camden was. "I don't want to hurt Bradley. I'm trying to help her. She's just too stubborn to realize it."

Camden glanced at his bedside clock and let out a whimper. With an unhappy look at the time, he shut off the alarm that was due to go off soon, giving up on the ten minutes of sleep he still should have had. He then trudged over to his closet and started riffling through its contents. "Maybe she just doesn't like you," he offered.

Beau's eyes narrowed at Camden's lack of helpfulness. "She likes me plenty," he half growled. "Trust me."

"Maybe she was just being friendly," Camden continued, pulling out a pair of frayed corduroy pants. "She's not the type to be mean...even if the person deserves it," he added, giving Beau a pointed look.

"There was nothing *just friendly* about the way she was kissing me," Beau shot back. "There was real attraction there." Just the memory of her soft body pressed firmly against his had his mind thinking things of the carnal persuasion.

"Oh, that?" Camden asked, waving Beau off. "That was just to get Carter off her back. I wouldn't look too much into that."

"Then why didn't she kiss you, Camden?" Beau asked, voice smug. "She chose me because she likes me." He eyed Camden critically for a moment. "Better than you at least," he felt the need to add.

After a moment in which Beau let Camden mull over that probability, he said, "Also, as nice as that kiss was, that wasn't the time I was referring to." He shot Camden a superior look, his expression implying that he'd just won this battle.

Camden's green eyes widened in surprise. "Bradley? My Bradley? Kissing a relative stranger? Again? That...that's just not like her." He set Beau with a suspicious look. "What have you done to her?"

Beau chose not to answer. He found things to be quite the opposite. What had Bradley done to him, making him second-guess his tactics? *Get in. Kill. Get out.* That had always been his motto. Now, he was seducing a hit and bunking with her playschool buddy. How had he degraded his standards so quickly?

Trying to ignore what his actions could possibly be hinting at, Beau grumbled, "Just tell me how I can get in touch with her."

"On a Monday morning?" Camden asked. "Impossible. She volunteers at the crisis hotline on Monday mornings."

Beau arched an eyebrow. "A lot of business on Monday mornings?"

Camden nodded with a grimace. "'Fraid so. People tend to party hard over the weekend and panic for their Monday morning exams. It's a hectic job, but Bradley handles it pretty well."

"She's a saint, isn't she?" Beau asked, a little snidely.

"Pretty much," Camden agreed, picking up a toiletry bag and sliding into a pair of slippers.

"Give me the number," Beau demanded.

With a roll of his big, green eyes, Camden grabbed a pamphlet off his desk. "Here," he said, handing the paper over so Beau could get a look at it. "You can't call her, though. It's for emergencies and advice."

"Watch me," Beau said, dismissing him.

Camden froze in the doorway. "If you call her there, she's going to know I told you she would be there, and then she'll kill me."

Beau had the cordless phone in his hand. He paused briefly, eyeing Camden. "That's a risk I'm willing to take."

Camden shook his head in disappointment and left the room.

As soon as Camden was gone, Beau dialed the hotline number.

A moment later, Bradley's voice came across the line. "Campus Help Line."

"Hello, Bradley."

There was a pause and he just knew she was frowning. "Um...this is an anonymous line. I...I didn't give you my name."

"I'm not too keen on Bradley," Beau continued. "It's a boy's name. It confuses people because you most decidedly are not at all manish."

"Ummm, thanks...I think."

"What is your middle name? Something girly?"

"Isabella," she said tentatively.

"Isabella. Lovely. I do think I will call you Bella."

"Is...is this Mr. Channing?"

"I'm *Mr. Channing* now?" With a throaty chuckle, Beau said, "After last night I think we should definitely be on a first name basis."

"Last night..." She broke off and lowered her voice as if she was worried someone around her might hear. "Last night was my way of getting rid of you. I let you have your 'freebie' kiss so you would leave me alone. With that out of the way, we have no further business."

Beau felt his temper rise at the nonchalant way she dismissed him. No one had ever treated him with such a lack of fear. "We are not finished with our business. You still have my artifact. I won't back down, Miss Hildebrand," he said, throwing as much sarcasm as he could into the formal use of her name.

"You've got a lot of nerve, Mr. Channing," she tossed back with just as much heat in her voice.

Ignoring her, Beau pressed on. "Furthermore, you claim that kiss was just a simple repayment. You and I both know

that's a total lie. I never would have forced something so ridiculous on you and you know it." His voice lowered, becoming husky and seductive. "You know what I am. You know
that I could hear your heart pounding in your chest whenever I touched you. I can sense your attraction to me. Don't
lie to me about this just being a way to break even with me."

"There you go with the vampire thing again," she
snapped. "I'm not stupid! I know you're not a vampire."

"Are you using the topic of my undead status as an excuse to ignore how much my last statement rang true?" Beau
asked wickedly, taking delight in the memory of the way her
breathing had hitched before she distracted herself with the
vampire denial she was still clinging to.

"You're not a vampire," she repeated.

"How can you deny what I am when you saw the proof
for yourself last night?"

"What I saw," Bradley said tersely, "was an elaborate
magic trick. One, I would like to add, that I didn't appreciate.
You cut my lip up for a hoax. It's rude, and you did not ask
for my permission."

"I nicked your tongue," Beau said after a little growl of
frustration. "It wasn't intentional. I haven't-" He broke off,
not wanting to admit the rest of his sentence.

"You haven't what?" Bradley asked, sounding intrigued
despite her attempts not to be.

"It's been a long time since I've had to try to kiss around
a mouthful of fangs, okay?"

Her voice softened. "Why's that?"

"Because I'd become jaded. I was appalled with the way
humanity behaved. Everyone's either out to kill each other or
cheat someone out of money. There isn't any loyalty left out
there anymore. The women...the last few women I was with
were, excuse the pun, the nail in my coffin. I lost all attraction to, well, anyone," he admitted, letting out an irritated
huff, "which has really put me in a sucky position."

Bradley giggled.

Beau grinned despite the seriousness of what he was
about to confess to her. "I heard that. Do you find something
about my word choice humorous?"

"Yeah," she came back in amusement. "You're in a *sucky*
position. Aren't vampires *always* in sucky positions?"

"Usually," Beau said, his tone warm. "Only I've been having some trouble with the sucking."

"Didn't seem so last night," Bradley commented, a teasing note in her voice.

"That's the problem!" he cried. With a sigh, he added, "Let me explain this to you." When she didn't protest, he continued. "Feeding is normally a very intimate act, almost sexual. A vampire's fangs only extend when..." He trailed off with a grimace, not really wanting to talk about this with her.

"When he's turned on?" Bradley guessed. "Kind of like..." It was her turn to trail off in embarrassment.

Beau envisioned her cheeks flushing pink due to the taboo subject. This brought a small smile to his lips. "That's it exactly. They appear in times of arousal. The only other time they surface is in confrontational situations. They're kind of like a defense mechanism."

"Basically during times of very strong emotion," Bradley ventured. "They show up regardless of whether the emotion is good or bad."

Beau gave a careless shrug even though she couldn't see it. "I suppose that's one way to look at it." He leaned back against Camden's desk, striking a casual pose as the kid came back into the room fresh and changed from his shower.

Seeing the phone in Beau's hand, Camden shook his head in disgust.

Beau shot him a dirty look, but continued his conversation as if Camden wasn't there. "When I lost my appetite for human intercourse, it raised a few problems in terms of feeding myself."

Though it seemed impossible, Camden's look became more appalled. "What are you telling her?"

"Luckily my fangs sort of evolved. They learned to extend without me being...you know. They worked because it was vital to my survival. I've been feeding that way, without the need of arousal, for quite some time now."

"Okay," Bradley said slowly. "Lucky you...I suppose."

"Up until last night I was," he grumbled. "Things were working perfectly fine until I went and got the hots for you," he complained. "Last night you brought my fangs out through sexual attraction."

"Well, that's the way they're supposed to work." Her voice sounded as if she was merely humoring him. "It's their natural instinct."

"Yeah, but you sent me away hungry." He let out a frustrated grunt. "I tried feeding off of someone else after I left your place last night, but I couldn't get my fangs to cooperate. It's because they know I'm attracted to you! They're refusing to work the other way. Because of you, I'm starving!"

"I don't know if you're complimenting me or yelling at me," Bradley admitted.

"Neither do I!"

Camden's eyebrows rose. "She is so gonna kill me."

Beau spun on him with a snarl. "Get to class!"

"Yikes," Camden cried. "All right, Dracula," he said sarcastically.

"And now you've made me reveal my secret in front of Camden! Before yesterday, no human has *ever* known about me!"

"Well, maybe you should learn to keep your undead mouth shut," she suggested.

Beau spun to point a finger at Camden, Bradley's comment inspiring him to tell the kid the same thing. "You keep your mouth *shut* or I will rip your head off and make a feast of the fountain of blood that pours from your neck."

"You really are a felon," Camden said with a grimace as he slung his book bag over one shoulder. "And not just like petty vandalism. You're doing crazy Jeffery Dahmer shit."

"That's right I am! You'd be wise to keep that in mind!" Beau hollered to the closing door.

"Don't threaten Camden," Bradley chastised.

"I'm just keeping things in perspective," Beau reasoned.

"Drinking a fountain of his blood and dancing over his decapitated body is in no way keeping things in perspective."

"I never said anything about dancing," Beau pointed out, his eyebrows rising at her gross exaggeration.

"Poor Camden's afraid of the dark! What do you think threatening him...Hey!" she cried, voice thick with accusation. "It's light out! The sun is up and so are you! That right there proves that you most definitely *aren't* a vampire."

"Bella, I am not in a speedo lounging in front of the pool while I speak to you. The sun is just now peeking through the sky. I am well hidden in Camden's room with the blinds tightly drawn," he informed her as he did just that, making sure to block out even the slightest possibility of sunlight.

"Don't you need a coffin or something?" Bradley asked in

curiosity. "And don't call me Bella."

He let out a huffy sigh. "A coffin? Honestly." Rolling his eyes, he said, "What I need is something to keep me amused while I'm stuck here. Do you know how boring daytime television is?"

"Why don't you sleep? Haven't you been up all night?"

"Can't sleep," Beau came back. "For one, I'm distracted by the fact that I can't eat. Also, I need to come up with a plan to avoid the disasters that are bound to arise when the bad guys find out you have that artifact."

"That should keep you busy then, shouldn't it?" she snapped.

"You could come keep me company when you get done. That would keep me entertained," Beau ventured, his voice low and husky. "It could also help with the hunger issue."

After an uncomfortable pause, Bradley said, "I need to get off the phone."

"Why?" Beau demanded, his voice holding an edge of challenge to it. "Because you like the idea of feeding me?"

"Because this is a help line for *students*, Mr. Channing. Seeing as how you are neither a student, nor a professor, you aren't permitted to be using this line."

"Are you saying you'd turn away someone in dire need just because they aren't a student? You would deny me assistance because of a technicality? How helpful is that?"

"You aren't in need of any help," Bradley scoffed. After a thoughtful pause, she added, "Well, mental help perhaps, but I fear you need a true professional."

"How do you know I'm not going to walk out into the sunlight over the stress of this situation?"

"You said yourself you've done this before. After a few hundred years of dealing with the stress of your job, I'm confident you'll be just fine," she reasoned. "Good-bye, Mr. Channing."

"Listen to me, Bradley," Beau said, lowering his voice in warning. "All jokes and feelings I have for you aside, I must get that necklace. I will do whatever necessary to obtain it. I like you, little Bella, but I will not let innocent mortals die because of your stubbornness. Do not make me relieve you of that artifact by force. I don't want to hurt you..." He trailed off, leaving the "but" of that sentence left unsaid.

"Goodbye, Mr. Channing," was her cold reply. "Don't contact me again."

Beau heard the line go dead, heard her hang up on him, but still he whispered, "I wish it was as easy as that, little Bella. I truly wish it was."

Chapter 5

Beau had been pretending to watch some sitcom rerun for the past twenty minutes, but his eyes were trained on the blinds.

The sun was setting. Another reason to love the fall, the sun began setting earlier and earlier.

The door clicked open, but Beau barely spared it a glance once he confirmed that it was Camden.

"So how'd the phone call go?" Camden asked, tiredly dropping his backpack to the ground.

Beau sent him an annoyed look. "I'm here on my own. How do you think it went?"

"Well, telling her you were a vampire surely didn't help," Camden commented, giving Beau a look that clearly said he thought Beau was crazy.

"I thought I told you never to mention that!" Beau snarled, leaping to his feet.

Camden held his hands up. "Sorry. Jeez." He rolled his eyes and snorted, turning his back on Beau as he went to the mini-refrigerator that sat between the two beds in the room. "Apparently vampires are touchy creatures."

Beau's shoulders bunched in irritation at the way Camden so casually turned his back to him. He was a vampire! He'd made his living as an assassin. He'd viciously and heartlessly killed hundreds of people. Beau had the urge to snap Camden's arrogant little neck. The kid needed to learn to show some respect.

Before Beau could do that, Camden spun back around and plopped down on the bed to the left, opening the bottle of water he held in his hands. "So what's the plan now?"

Beau climbed to his feet, a look of determination on his face. "I'm going to her place."

Camden's brows drew together. "I don't think she's going to like you showing up unannounced like that."

"I'm hoping she won't be there," Beau returned. "I'm going to have to turn her apartment upside down to find that necklace. Things will probably go smoother if she's not there while I'm doing it."

"Okay," Camden said slowly. "She's *definitely* not going to like that." It took his tired mind a moment to really comprehend what Beau intended to do. "You're going to ransack her place?"

"Yeah," Beau said wearily, making his way to the door.

"She's not going to like that one bit."

"No. She isn't." Beau closed the door, shutting out any further comments Camden planned to make. He didn't need the kid to tell him how invasive this was, or what a bad guy he was. He'd been doing this for years. Funny how it had never bothered him before he'd met Bradley and Camden.

Beau was just exiting the hallway and stepping into the lobby of the dormitory when something in the far corner caught his eye. Cursing under his breath, he slid back into the shadowed hall.

Jordan Craven, renowned dark wizard and practitioner of the dark arts, stood in front of a nervous-looking student. He was obviously grilling the kid, searching for information on the whereabouts of Bradley.

So Craven had made the same assumption about Bradley being a boy. Good.

Beau knew that Craven was searching for Bradley because he'd had run-ins with the spoiled, over privileged heir to a candy factory before. He knew how Craven operated and what type of items he usually went for. Craven was continuously searching for more power, more recognition. If he'd heard even the slightest rumor that the artifact Bradley had could be in the area, he'd have the best supernatural snoops on it.

Jordan had short, spiked blond hair and eyes the color of ice that, when looked into, were cold and calculating. He usually wore business suits, giving him a wealthy and professional look. It was easier to dupe people into giving you information you needed that way.

Last time Beau and Jordan had sought the same item, six people ended up dead, one of them Jordan's younger brother.

Beau knew that there was no love lost between him and Craven. It had been made completely clear when Jordan had vowed to avenge his brother's death and see Beau on the sharp end of a stake. That had been six months ago, and now here they were, tracking down another item at the same time.

"Damn," Beau grumbled, then soundlessly began making his way back up the hall to Camden's room. The door opened just as he reached it, and Beau shoved past a startled look-ing Camden and shut the door behind him.

After blinking in surprise for a few seconds, Camden said, "Oh, good. I'm glad you changed your mind. I was just on my way out to stop you."

Beau slid him a cool, appraising look. "As if you could." Before Camden could respond, he continued. "The plan has changed."

"Plan? I wasn't aware there was a plan," Camden replied a little warily.

"The plan is not to get killed," Beau snapped.

"That wasn't the plan before?"

Beau spun on him with a snarl, flashing a mouthful of fangs.

Camden's eyes widened in shock and he stumbled back-wards, sinking down to the bed when it hit the back of his knees. "Holy shit!" he cried in disbelief. "You've got fangs!"

Beau's lip curled into a wry grin. "That tends to happen when I'm angry." He set Camden with a serious look, all amusement leaving his face. "Listen up, kid. There are men downstairs that are after Bradley. They would put a bullet in the back of her head without giving it a second thought. Lucky for us, I think they made the same error I did in think-ing Bradley was a boy. It won't buy us much time before they realize this error, but it will give us some."

Camden looked completely overwhelmed. "Why would someone want to hurt Bradley?"

"Because she's got a very powerful item in her posses-sion, an item those men would kill for."

Realization spread across Camden's face. "That's why you showed up, isn't it? For the item."

"Yeah," Beau said softly, "but I'm not looking to use it for personal gain. I wanted to hide it so it didn't fall into the wrong hands." His jaw clenched in anger. "Only Bradley wouldn't give it up."

"You have to earn Bradley's trust. She doesn't just hand it out to anyone," Camden said gruffly, coming to his best friend's defense. "She probably didn't know if she could trust you."

"Time's up for that now. Either she trusts me or she's going to get herself killed."

"They know she has it, though," Camden reminded him. "At this point, won't they kill her anyway? Even if she gets rid of it by giving it to you?"

"Shit," Beau swore under his breath, running a hand through his hair. He hadn't thought of that. He'd never left someone alive before for the bad guys to get a hold of. Trying to keep a fragile mortal... Beau glanced at Camden. He realized that Camden was also now under his protection. He couldn't let anything happen to Bradley's best friend because the guilt of feeling responsible for whatever happened to Camden would kill her. Beau corrected his previous train of thought. Trying to keep *two* mortals alive, let alone one, had never been a concern of his.

Camden was right, though. Craven would kill Bradley once he tracked her down regardless of whether she still had the artifact or not. "What options do I have, though?" Beau quietly asked himself. "Spirit Bradley away and keep her with me for the rest of eternity?"

His heart, which was used to no longer beating, gave an excited thump at that idea. Surprised, Beau put a hand to his chest, feeling another dull beat under his palm. Just the thought of Bradley had his body reacting in ways he hadn't believed still possible. He'd heard rumors of vampires whose hearts would beat when they felt strong emotions, but he'd thought it to be a myth.

As much as the idea of keeping Bradley for himself appealed to him now, Beau needed to look at the long run. He couldn't drag a college kid out of her life and expect her to give up everything she knew. Besides, he'd been on his own for so long that he didn't know if he could change his entire way of living, even if it was for Bradley. He couldn't imagine spending the next eighty years with Camden yapping in his ear. "I'm going to have to kill Craven," he finally realized. "Once and for all, it's going to end."

Chapter 6

Beau stared at the phone in his hand in disbelief. "She hung up on me."

After coming to the understanding that he was going to have to kill Jordan Craven, Beau had gone through a rough plan with Camden. He felt it necessary to warn Camden about how dangerous the situation was. Beau staying in Camden's room and the fact that the two of them had probably been seen together meant the bad guys would most likely think Camden was Bradley. To Beau's surprise, Camden didn't mind.

Camden had said he hoped the bad guys continued to think this so they wouldn't go after the real Bradley.

The kid had earned respect in Beau's eyes for the way he was willing to put himself in danger to protect his best friend.

After their discussion, they both agreed that warning Bradley was the first step of action.

Beau had immediately dialed the cell phone number Camden handed him only to have Bradley hang up on him the moment she recognized his voice.

"*What* did you say to her this morning?" Camden asked in accusation.

Beau's face flashed impatience before he grudgingly said, "That I would get the artifact from her by force if I had to."

Camden shook his head, giving Beau a reproachful look. "No wonder she won't talk to you."

Beau shoved the phone into Camden's hand. "Reason with her."

Camden took the phone from Beau with a skeptical look on his face. "Bradley's usually cool and all, but she's still a woman. There's no reasoning with that."

"Try," Beau said dryly, though he struggled not to

chuckle at Camden's comment.

Looking reluctant, Camden hit redial and waited for Bradley to answer. When her agitated voice came over the line, he quickly said, "Brad, it's Camden. Don't hang up."

Beau could hear shrill shouting coming from Bradley's end and assumed she was yelling at Camden for giving him her cell phone number.

"Honey, calm down!" Camden cried, cringing as he held the phone out to protect his eardrum.

Beau's lip pulled into a frown at the pet name.

Camden put the phone back to his ear. He listened for a moment before saying, "Well, he looks totally jealous and ready to tear my head off for calling you honey." After another pause, he cried, "Of *course* I walked away from him before saying that. I wouldn't let him know that you were asking about him." To Beau, he rolled his eyes and mouthed, *Women.*

Bradley said something on the other line, and he rolled his eyes again. "Yes. He looks unbelievably sexy. He's been walking around in his underwear all morning. I can hardly keep my eyes off of him."

There was a brief pause, then Camden huffed, "Of course I'm not serious. Can we forget about his underwear and move on to the importants? You really need to talk to him. You need to hear what he has to tell you."

Camden began smacking his feet against the floor, feigning walking. "I'm on my way over to him now. Okay, hold on..." Moving the phone away from his ear, he informed Beau, "Bradley wants me to let you know that she thinks you're a dick."

Beau's cocky, pleased smirk fell. Sending Camden a dirty look, he snatched the phone from his hands. "Listen to me, little Bella..."

Bradley cut him off. "Don't call me that. My name is not Bella, and I am five foot nine. Stop calling me little."

"Compared to me you are little," Beau reasoned. "And to me, you are my little Bella. The nickname suits you. Sweet, feminine, and dainty."

There was a pause in which Beau knew she was struggling over whether to feel agitated or delighted. Finally, not wishing to respond to that comment at all, she said, "What lies have you been filling Camden's head with? What stories did you invent to get him so freaked out?"

Beau sighed. "I have never lied to you, little Bella. Not once, even though I know I should have from the very beginning. It would have been safer for you."

"Fine," she grumbled, obviously not wishing to debate about the vampire issues again. "What did you need to tell me?"

Beau knew she wasn't going to like, or easily believe, what he was about to say, but he had little choice at this point. "There are some men downstairs in Camden's lobby that are looking for you. If they find you, they will kill you." He waited a beat, letting that information sink in. "If you are in your room, you need to leave it. Unless I am with you, it is not safe for you to be there." Unable to help himself and the shameless flirt he'd become, he let a wicked grin touch his lips as he asked, "Are you going to be moving me in?"

"No," she said coldly.

"Then you need to leave. Grab your necklace and go somewhere you feel safe. Don't tell anyone where you are going, not even me. Just call Camden when you get there and let him know you're all right."

"Not you?" she asked in a soft, angelic voice. "You aren't concerned with my safety?"

Beau wouldn't have been able to stop the lopsided grin that spread across his face if he tried. "I had every intention of answering the phone."

"Oh," she whispered in a breathy, pleased voice. "Okay. I'll go."

"Okay? That's it?" he asked in surprise. "No arguments?"

"I thought about it, but you sound genuinely concerned. Besides, I'm done with all of my classes for the day. It wouldn't inconvenience me too much to stay with a friend tonight."

Beau hated the jealous sound in his voice and his need to ask, "Your friend is female?"

Bradley's reply held amusement. "My friend is female," she confirmed.

"Well," he said gruffly, trying to move away from the topic of her *female* friend, "Get to it. Camden and I have work to do that we can't start until we hear from you."

Camden looked up from the stack of mail he was sorting through. "We do?" On Beau's glare, he silenced any further protests he was about to make. "That's right. We do," he agreed lamely, the tone of his voice giving away how little he looked forward to whatever it was Beau wanted him to do.

Beau returned his attention back to the phone. "And Bradley, be careful."

"I will," came her shaky, nervous reply.

He could tell she wanted to say more, so he waited. He'd just filled her in on a very scary situation, so he could understand if it took her a little time to get her thoughts in order.

"Beau?" she finally ventured, her voice reluctant.

"Yes?" he asked gently, his voice full of patience.

There was a long pause before she finally said, "Don't let anything bad happen to Camden."

"I won't," Beau promised.

There was another pause where he could tell she was debating on voicing what she wanted to say. After a moment of silence, she gave in and added, "You be careful, too."

Beau heard the click of her hastily hanging up the phone. He spun to face Camden with a crooked, pleased grin. "Told you she liked me," he said, tossing the phone back to its skeptical-looking owner.

Camden raised a questioning eyebrow as he placed the phone back on the receiver. "How do you figure?"

"She told me to be careful."

Camden rolled his eyes with a snort. "You are really grasping at straws, buddy."

Beau gave him a dirty look, but unfortunately, they were having less and less effect on the kid.

Instead, Camden's grin grew.

"You won't think it's funny when I eat you," Beau grumbled.

Camden simply threw back his head and laughed.

Chapter 7

Two hours later, Beau and Camden sat in Camden's beat up Grand Am. They were parked across the street from a group of poorly maintained lawns, so Camden's car fit right in. Two blocks down was an abandoned warehouse they'd tracked one of Craven's men to. Beau and Camden had been sitting inside the car for the past twenty minutes surveying for any activity.

Beau was thankful Camden had managed to remain relatively silent so far. He didn't think he could handle a stakeout filled with the kid's nonstop chatter.

"I'm still worried we're going to get mugged," Camden fretted, breaking up the silence. "We aren't exactly in the best part of town."

Beau suppressed a groan. He knew the quiet was too good to last. "We aren't going to get mugged."

"You don't know that for sure. Five minutes ago, I saw a group of thugs with baseball bats a block behind us."

"You mean the baseball team of junior high kids?" Beau asked with a smirk. "Yeah, they were real dangerous," he said sarcastically. His eyes still trained on the warehouse, he said, "Besides, you're with a vampire. Do you think a few baseball bats are going to do much damage?"

"I guess not," Camden said reluctantly. "Unless they splinter and stab you in the heart."

Beau spared him a glance. "Bradley was right. You get spooked easily."

"Why...when...Bradley..." Camden sputtered. "Well..." Finally coming up with a coherent thought, he said, "Bradley wouldn't say that."

"She said you were afraid of the dark," Beau felt the need to add, his eyes sparkling in amusement.

"I am not!" Camden cried, but couldn't stop the wary glance he sent out the window at the darkness.

"You're right. She must have just made it up."

Camden sulked for a couple of minutes in which Beau blissfully took in the silence. When he couldn't take it anymore, Camden grumbled, "That traitor. All it takes is one super hot vampire and she's selling me out."

"So..." Beau said slowly, trying to sound casual, "Bradley thinks I'm hot?"

Camden narrowed his eyes in agitation. "Don't give me innocent face. You know damn well how she feels. The poor girl's never behaved so irrationally over a guy before. It's like she's in love with you or something."

Beau's eyes narrowed in suspicion. "Why do you sound so unhappy about that? You don't have a crush on Bradley, do you?"

Camden snorted. "Hardly. She's not my type. I just worry about the fact that the only guy she's really ever liked in twenty years is a vampire. The odds of a disastrous outcome that will leave her heartbroken are phenomenal."

Beau frowned, not positive he could deny that statement. Instead, he asked, "What about Bradley don't you like? Why isn't she your type?"

Camden shrugged. "She's like my sister. We wore diapers together. We went through that pimply, awkward stage together."

"You mean *you* went through that pimply, awkward stage and she was still nice to you," Beau commented.

Camden sent him a sneer, but didn't deny it. After a moment, he continued, "Bradley's my girl. I love her. She's been there my entire life as my best friend. She's closer to me than my real sister. Where it counts, Bradley *is* my sister." He sent Beau a sly look. "It's always been a personal rule of mine to not make out with my sister."

"That's a good rule," Beau agreed.

"I thought so," Camden said smoothly. "Besides, I've had my eyes on Kristie Taylor for the past year and a half." On Beau's confused look, he added, "The blond with Bradley's ex?"

"Ah, yes." Beau sent him another quick glance. "Her breasts are artificial," he said, sounding almost concerned.

"Okay?" Camden asked with a laugh.

"That is something you find attractive?"

"I find the whole package attractive. I'd like to cover her in strawberry syrup and whip cream and..." He trailed off at Beau's look.

"You're disgusting," Beau informed him. As an after-thought, he added, "Bradley's breasts look authentic. I believe I like them."

"And you say *I'm* disgusting," Camden griped. "I don't sit around talking about *your* sister's boobs."

Beau gave a casual shrug. "My sister's been dead nearly four hundred years. I'm past being insulted by sister jokes."

Camden's blond brows drew together. "You're, like, to-tally old. Ancient even."

Beau rolled his eyes before sending Camden a crooked grin. "That doesn't stop your sister from thinking I'm hot."

"You know, for a vampire, you're a real smart ass."

Beau's smirk widened. "The rest of my kind seems to think so, as well." After a moment of mutual chuckling, his face grew serious. "I don't think they're going to be doing anything else tonight," Beau said with a glance at the de-signer watch on his left wrist. "Craven's hired muscle tends to be vampires. Every once in a while he'll pick up a werewolf or two, but I don't think we'll have much to worry about with them. Werewolves and other shifters similar to them are usually assigned to the less violent crimes. The vampires are the ones that do the dirtier work."

He paused thoughtfully. "Werewolves are also very hard to find. They don't sell their morals as easily as vampires do. They, on a whole, tend to be normal people with a fun, little secret, not cold-blooded killers who need to feed off others to survive. That bottom-feeding existence of death and gore is saved for my kind, the kind that would kill their own mothers if it presented monetary gain."

"Good to know you can be trusted," Camden said, his voice full of apprehension.

Beau turned in his seat to give Camden the full weight of his stare. "Yeah, we're real bastards."

By the frightened look on Camden's face, Beau figured his eyes must be blazing with anger, but he was too agitated to care. "You know what creature is more easily corrupted than a vampire?" Beau asked, his voice dark with fury. On Camden's silence, he answered, "Humans. Maybe it's the short life span. Perhaps it makes them need instant gratification. Whatever the reason, they'll sell out their own family for riches. The only reason Craven doesn't use them is because they break too easily. That and the fact that they arrogantly tend to deny that the rest of us exist. They don't like finding out they're at the bottom of our food chain."

Beau spun back around in his seat to face the road. "So perhaps it is I that should be suspecting you of treachery." He started the car up and began the drive back to Camden's, his jaw clenched and his face stony.

There was a minute of uncomfortable silence before Camden said, "I'm sorry. I didn't mean to imply that I didn't trust you. You've done nothing but try to keep me and Bradley safe." He sent Beau a goofy, lopsided grin. "Especially the way you protected me from that gang of twelve-year-old baseball players. They were a fearsome bunch."

Beau turned to stare at him in complete silence for a moment before bursting out into a deep, rich laugh. "For an incredibly weird and scraggly fellow, you're pretty funny." He laughed a moment longer, before adding, "You're welcome, by the way. It was a challenge, but I finally managed to overcome the pimple squad." He flashed a teasing grin.

"Scraggly and weird?" Camden asked, sounding shocked at the description. He quickly shrugged off the jab. "Well, for an evil, blood sucking fiend of the night, you're not so bad yourself...that is when you're not threatening to rip my head off and drink from the fountain of blood that pours forth."

Beau gave a noncommittal shrug. After a moment, his expression became serious again. "Craven and his men should be done for the rest of the night, seeing as the sun will be up in little over an hour. They're not going anywhere." He slid a quick glance to Camden before turning back to the road. "Get some sleep and I'll pick you up when the sun goes down, see if we can find out what they're up to."

Camden gave him a surprised look. "You're not imposing yourself at my place again?"

Beau shook his head. "No. There's a possibility we've already been spotted together. The more you're seen with me, the better the chances of Craven killing you because he thinks you're Bradley. Though his vampires will be indoors for the day, there's a chance he may have a shape-shifter or two following me. They'll be trailing me, not you. The farther away from me you are, the safer you'll be. These guys are too afraid to make a move without Craven's okay first, so they won't stray from the plan of keeping tabs on me to go after you. Just in case they haven't found me yet, I booked a room at a nearby hotel under a fake name. I'll stay there for the day and pick you up shortly after nightfall."

"So you're not staying, but you're taking my car?"

"Yes." Beau gave him an insipid look. "Is there a problem with that?"

Camden gave a lazy shrug, trying to look as nonchalant as Beau, but not pulling it off quite as well. "I just don't want you to keep it."

Beau's bored look turned into one of amusement. "You think I'd honestly want this hunk of junk? I've had a couple hundred years to accumulate money. I've got four different cars at home that cost more than your college education and you think I want this piece of scrap metal?"

Camden stammered over a reply, his cheeks flushing with embarrassment. "I...you...well..." Finally, he mumbled, "I'll see you when the sun goes down then."

"As long as I don't change my mind and take off with this beauty of a car," Beau taunted with a smug grin, rubbing a hand with mock fondness along the dashboard.

"Smart ass vampire," Camden grumbled, climbing out of the car.

As Camden went to walk away, Beau surprised him by setting him with a solemn stare. "Hey, kid. Be careful. Don't open your door to anyone besides me. If things get bad, just barricade your door until I get there at sundown."

Camden gulped, his Adam's apple bobbing in his throat. "You sure know how to freak a guy out."

"It was meant to," Beau came back. "One slip up and you're dead, and then Bradley probably is too. I'm just trying to make sure you realize that." His eyes studied Camden critically. "So don't do anything stupid." With that said, he peeled off.

Chapter 8

Beau parked Camden's car in the back of the hotel parking lot, trying to keep it in the shadows of the nearby trees so no one would notice it. The less attention he drew to himself, the better.

As he climbed out of the car, he gave a quick glance to the sky. Less than an hour left until sunrise. Over the years, he'd grown to resent the fact that he would never again feel the warm glow of the sun on his face, but tanning poolside was the least of his concerns at the moment. Picking up his pace, he walked toward the hotel, his mind distracted with drawing up a plan of action to carry out when he was no longer confined to the shadows.

That's why he didn't notice the man that crept up behind him with a lead pipe until the weapon connected with the back of his head.

Beau stumbled and dropped to one knee from the force of the blow. He felt cool air on his scalp as if a breeze was blowing on the spot he'd been hit. He knew it meant the back of his head had been busted open and that he'd been hurt badly. He also knew that he was lucky he wasn't human, because whoever had swung the pipe surely wasn't.

He struggled to his feet, his eyes glued to his assailant. He immediately categorized him as a werewolf, though the man was still in human form. Shifters stood out in a crowd of supernatural creatures like a sore thumb. They spent more effort on trying to appear human than vampires tended to.

While Beau sized him up, the shifter prepared for his next attack.

This time, when the shifter came at him, Beau was ready. He ducked the pipe and reached out to his assailant's neck. His fingers closed around an Adam's apple and he pulled, ripping the werewolf's throat out.

Beau heard the person gurgling for air as they hit the ground, but he didn't get a good look at his attacker's face because he was suddenly hit in the temple with a two by four. Stars exploded behind his eyes and blood instantaneously began to trail down his face.

He staggered, but didn't go down. He couldn't afford to. There were seven men currently surrounding him. The werewolf, who would make eight, was kneeling nearby on the ground, cradling his slowly reforming throat. At least he'd be out for a little while.

Beau eyed up the other seven men through blood soaked eyes. Five vampires, two humans. Once the werewolf's throat healed over, it would be back on the attack. It would eventually be eight on one. Not exactly the best odds.

In the instant it took him to survey his attackers, the man with the two by four was bringing it back around for another swing.

Beau barely managed to do a diving roll out of the way. Unfortunately, he was forced to roll into the feet of another one of his attackers. Something blunt slammed into the back of his already wounded head.

Less than a second later, another person's booted foot connected with his gut.

Beau tried to avoid the next blow, but there were just too many coming from every angle. He had seven men simultaneously striking him.

A wooden baseball bat slammed into his back so violently that it shattered into four pieces.

Using the little opportunity he had, Beau grabbed one of the shards and stabbed it into the closest knee.

There was a howl of pain and one of the vampires backed off.

This gave Beau the opportunity to grab one of the humans by the front of his shirt. With a snarl, he dragged the man down to the pavement with him. Before anyone could realize what he was doing, Beau lifted the man's head, then drove his skull down onto the blacktop.

There was the satisfying sound of the man's skull caving in before the remaining five men all swooped in on Beau.

Beau couldn't take all of them at once. There were just too many and he wasn't at full strength because he hadn't fed recently. Also, he was losing too much blood. A mortal would have been out by now, but he fought back the blackness around the edge of his vision, trying to force himself not to lose consciousness. If he fainted, he wouldn't be waking up again. His attackers would see to that.

It didn't take long for them to overpower him. They didn't even bother taking turns like stereotypical bad guys. Instead, they all kicked and punched him in unison for all they were worth, not even giving him a chance to fight back.

Beau hunched over on the ground while they beat and pummeled him, curling into the fetal position to protect against as many blows as possible. If they messed up one of his eyes or broke something necessary to fight back, he was dead. The only thing that brought him any satisfaction was the wide, lifeless gaze of the human next to him on the pavement. If he was going to die, at least he'd taken one of them with him.

"Beau Channing," one of the men drawled. "It appears your reputation has been no more than exaggerations and fairy tales. I expected more of a fight."

"It's Beauregard," Beau said darkly. He somehow found the energy to spit blood out at the man's feet. "And you can go to hell."

The guy laughed in delight. "But they did not exaggerate about your personality." He turned to one of the men next to him. "Chain him up."

A second man came forward with a chain and padlock to assist the first.

Kicking and fighting, Beau was dragged by the two vampires backwards to the tree that was hidden behind his car. They chained him to the base of it, making sure he had as little mobility of his limbs as possible.

Once they had him restrained, one of the vampires forced Beau's face toward the man in charge. The vampire's long fingers dug into Beau's flesh, his power held in check just under the surface. It silently warned Beau of what could be done to him if he struggled.

Beau had no choice but to look at the man. He recognized him immediately as Kelvin Smith, one of Craven's loyal stooges. Kelvin and Jordan Craven had gone to school together, becoming interested in the dark arts because they'd had nothing better to do with their over privileged human

existences. Now Craven was running a following of supernatural lackeys, using them to increase his power in the
paranormal world. There was nothing Beau hated more than
humans that tried to control a posse of supernatural beings.
It was like a mouse trying to run a pack of stray cats. The
mouse would always end up getting eaten alive, but until this
mouse slipped up, he would be a pain in Beau's ass.

"Now, Beau," Kelvin said, clasping his hands in front of
him. "Where is Bradley?" He motioned for the vampire to
take a step back from Beau, his expression one of complete
patience.

Beau leaned his head against the tree trunk and stared
up at Kelvin. He took a deep, ragged breath that sent pain
racing though his rib cage. "If you think I'm telling you jack
shit, you're out of your mind."

Kelvin's hands balled into fists. He gave a quick nod to
the vampire. "Conrad," he said smoothly.

The vampire stepped forward and dutifully cracked Beau
across the face with his fist.

"Why are you protecting some punk kid? Tell us where he
is and we'll let you go."

A small grin tugged at Beau's lips. So they hadn't figured
out that Bradley was a girl. He would happily die keeping
that secret. He'd rather die in excruciating pain than hand
over Bradley and have a quick death. For now, at least, she
was still safe. He only hoped that she and Camden would be
able to piece things together when he didn't return and have
enough brains to run. Kelvin didn't seem to think Camden
was Bradley. That meant Craven's men hadn't been tracking
Beau closely enough to link him to Camden. The kid was safe
for the moment, as well, safe enough to put distance between himself and Craven's men.

"What are you smiling about?" Kelvin snapped, his thin
face flushing with anger.

"The fact that you are completely clueless." Beau sent
Kelvin an arrogant smirk, a smirk that said he knew something the other man didn't. "What makes you think Bradley's
even still alive?"

"The fact that you're still here. You never stick around
after a kill."

"Maybe I haven't found what I'm looking for yet."

Kelvin nodded to Conrad and Beau received another shot

to his jaw.

"Well, you'd better remember some useful information real quick, because if you don't, we're going to leave you here," Kelvin threatened. "The sun will be up in less than twenty minutes. You don't want to be out here when that happens."

"I don't know. It's been awhile since I've had a good tan," Beau managed to get out around his swollen lip and a mouthful of blood.

"You're willing to die for some kid?" Kelvin asked incredulously.

Beau looked away, his eyes cold as he stared into the approaching dawn. "Bring on the sun."

Kelvin was staring in speculation at Beau when the werewolf whose throat had been ripped out jumped to its feet and threw himself at Beau.

Though the shifter was still in human form, his claws and teeth extended, both becoming razor sharp with the man's rage. He clawed at Beau's chest, ripping away a large chunk of flesh.

With a groan of pain, Beau attempted to hunch over and protect himself, but was unable to do much with his hands chained behind his back.

The shifter tore and scratched at his skin in a rage, elongated teeth gnashing dangerously near Beau's face. The only thing that kept the man from ripping Beau's nose off was the fact that he was distracted with trying to tear his organs out. A claw sliced across Beau's face, tearing through his cheek. Blood began to pour down his face in a thick line, trailing down his neck to soak into his shirt.

Beau turned his head to the side, trying to protect his torn flesh from the next slash of claws. The shifter's next swing hit him in the ear, splitting his skin painfully.

"Arliss! Arliss!" Kelvin said with a chuckle. "Calm yourself." His wicked grin widened. "The sun is a much more painful way to go."

"Are you going to stand there all day, or are you going to leave me to my horrible, fiery demise," Beau asked in a bored voice, not sounding at all concerned at the thought of being burned alive by the sun. "Because, frankly, I'm tired of listening to you."

Kelvin sneered down at him. "You're a fool, Beau, and

you'll die for it." He kicked dirt in Beau's face before turning and striding away. "It was nice knowing you."

Beau sat in patient silence on the ground until every member of Craven's crew had disappeared. As soon as they were out of eyesight, he began to tug at the chains, testing their durability. Had he been at full strength, he might have been able to snap them, but Kelvin had seen to that. Beau knew he was bleeding too heavily to have much strength, and the werewolf had ripped through the muscle on his left arm to the point that he could barely move it. He needed help, and he needed it fast.

Struggling with the uncooperative chains, Beau reached into his pocket and managed to close his hand around his cell phone. He couldn't lift it up due to the chains, but he was able to press the buttons with the phone still in his pocket. Moving by memory, he got it to the voice dial option. He almost demanded it to call Camden when he remembered that he had the kid's car. "Damn," Beau grumbled, realizing there was only one other choice. Almost reluctantly, he said, "Bradley."

"Did you say, 'Charlie'?" an electronic voice came back.

Beau gritted his teeth, forcing back the string of obscenities that would do him no good. "No," he seethed. "I said, Bradley," he repeated, trying to keep his cool.

"Did you say, 'Charlie'?" the phone repeated.

"Damn you!" Beau roared. "No! Bradley! Bradley!"

"Did you say, 'Bradley'?"

"Yes!" Beau cried in excitement. "Yes!" Shifting impatiently while it dialed, he thumbed through the options until he turned on the speakerphone, waiting for her to answer.

A moment later, muffled through his pocket, Bradley said, "Damn it, Beau! I was asleep! Just because you're a freak and stay up all night long does not mean the rest of us do. I did what you asked. I'm staying with a friend. What more do you want?"

Beau was glad the phone wasn't against his ear because that rant would have deafened him. "Bradley, sweetie," he soothed, trying to get her to calm down.

"Don't call me sweetie! I am not your sweetie!" she snapped.

"Fine. Pain in my ass, listen up," Beau griped. There was a small squawk of indignation on her end, but he ignored it.

"I'm in a...sticky situation. I need you to come get me at the Holiday Inn down the block from the college. If you don't get here before the sun rises, I'm going to die, so I suggest you hurry." A thought occurred to him, and he added, "Bring some bolt cutters."

"Where am I supposed to get bolt cutters?" she asked, sounding exasperated.

"I don't know," he said snidely. "How about try asking the superintendent? Or the hall monitor? Or whoever runs things where you are."

"All right. All right," she huffed. As an afterthought, she asked, "Where can I find you?"

"Chained to a tree in the back of the parking lot."

There was a brief pause where she mulled that over before saying, "I'm on my way."

Chapter 9

Bradley pulled into the Holiday Inn parking lot and threw her car into park. "How in the world did he manage to get chained to a tree?" she asked herself for the tenth time in the past fifteen minutes. "Where is he?" She stepped out of the car and searched the parking lot, finally spotting him at the back.

He was slouched against the base of a tree, hidden from plain sight behind Camden's car.

As she neared, she could see how badly injured he was.

Blood cascaded down Beau's forehead in rivulets. His face was twisted in an expression of pain, though he was trying to hide it. "Bradley," he hollered out to make sure she saw him.

"Beau!" she cried in horror, rushing over. "Oh my...what happened to you?"

"The men that want you dead. That's what happened. They were leaving me to be burned alive by the sun." He nodded down to the chains. "Get me out of here, will you?"

Bradley nodded frantically and lifted the bolt cutters to the lock holding the chains closed. With a little effort, she broke through the lock, causing the chains to slacken around Beau's chest. She didn't have time to celebrate this small victory because someone grabbed a handful of her hair and yanked her backwards.

"Kelvin was right," a voice snarled into her ear. "He led us right to you."

Bradley saw realization dawn in Beau's eyes.

"Damn it!" Beau hissed, struggling to get free of the chains still wrapped around him. "Let her go!" he roared.

The man tightened his grip in Bradley's hair, yanking her head back. "You must be pretty important for the legendary Beauregard Channing to be so concerned about you."

Another voice threw in, "Give us the artifact or she dies."

Beau finally managed to get to his feet. With lightning quick reflexes, he grabbed the man closest to him and tossed him into the tree he'd been chained against.

Bradley stood stunned for only a moment. She'd seen what these men had done to Beau and he had superhuman strength. They would kill her in an instant if they were given the opportunity. She wasn't going to just let them have her, though. If she was going to die, she was going to die fighting. Bringing her elbow back, Bradley slammed it into the gut of the man holding her. At the same time, she sunk her teeth into the arm he had wrapped around her upper chest.

The man gave a startled cry and released her, his initial reaction to free his arm from her teeth.

"Bradley!" Beau hollered. When she looked in his direction, he tossed her a splintered piece of a baseball bat. "You need to hit the heart!"

The meaning of his statement sunk in and Bradley fought not to panic. She'd never killed anyone before. She didn't know if she was capable of it.

While she stood frozen in uncertainty, Beau scooped up another piece of the bat. Spinning, he turned to face the group of men that were approaching him with caution. "Kelvin sent you guys back to do the dirty work while he hightailed it out of here," he growled out in disgust. One of them charged at him, and Beau slammed the jagged piece of wood through the man's chest.

The man didn't even have time to scream before his body disintegrated into dust.

Under his breath, Beau counted aloud, "Five of them left. Four vamps, one werewolf." He caught the makeshift stake as it fell. He then spun to block a blow from one of the other men. "Fight!" he growled to Bradley over his shoulder.

Bradley fearfully dragged her eyes back to the man that she'd elbowed free of only moments ago.

He now loomed over her with a smug look on his face.

In a panic at the savage demeanor of the vampire in from of her, Bradley shoved the broken piece of wood into his chest. It slid in half an inch, and then stopped.

The vampire stared down at the wood in his chest and let out a loud, degrading laugh. "You've got to use more force than that if you want to kill someone." He yanked the wood out and dropped it to the ground. The expression on his face said he didn't find her to be a threat at all. He thought she was an inferior being. He'd proven that by letting her attempt to stake him, knowing full well she would never be able to kill him.

His fingers twitched as if he was thinking about snapping her neck, but he paused and glanced at the fight going on over her shoulder, which apparently looked like more of a challenge. "I'll deal with you later," he promised, his gaze returning to Bradley, "but right now, I'm going to kill your boyfriend." Grabbing her shoulder, he shoved her roughly to the pavement.

Bradley hit the ground and was barely able to keep her skull from connecting with the concrete. Rocks dug viciously into her palms, embedding themselves in her skin. She didn't stop to examine them, though. These men were about to kill her and Beau. She couldn't afford to tend to her wounds. Staggering to her feet, she closed her fist around the make-shift stake she'd been given and started in Beau's direction.

Two men had Beau pinned to the ground and the vampire that had been holding her was ramming his boot down into his gut. They were all bent over and didn't see Bradley coming...or perhaps they simply didn't care.

She reached the group and stood directly behind the vampire that had tossed her to the ground. Lifting her arms over her head, she brought the shattered piece of baseball bat down as hard as she could.

The wood went nearly through the vampire's body. In shock, he attempted to straighten so he could turn and face his attacker. His movements helped drive the stake the rest of the way through his heart.

Bradley saw his startled, wide eyes before he turned to dust. She stumbled backwards in horror, her arms aching with the effort she'd used to kill the vampire. Before what she'd just done could fully sink in, arms wrapped around her from behind, pinning her arms to her sides. There was a feral growl and she could see fangs out of the corner of her eye.

On the ground, one of the men holding Beau down released his arm in surprise when his fellow henchman turned to dust.

As the body disintegrated, the stake fell through the dust. Beau caught it with his free hand and swiftly slammed it upward through the startled vampire's chest. "Two vampires, one werewolf," he said to himself, obviously liking those odds much better.

Before the vampire was even done turning to dust, Beau reached above his head, stretching to the tree he'd been tied to earlier. He grabbed onto the chain that had been used to restrain him. Sitting up, he seized the other man holding him down. Beau swiftly wrapped the chain around his neck, tightening it to crush the other man's windpipe.

The arms around Bradley jarred her around, but she still saw Beau snap the man's neck with the chain.

The man's head lulled lifelessly to the side, his eyes glazing over.

"Nice knowing you, Arliss," Beau jeered.

There were only the two vampires left now. One was a few feet in front of Beau and the other was holding Bradley.

Beau looked around thoughtfully. "I see Kelvin didn't return for this. Too scared to die with the rest of you?"

Enraged at Beau's comment and the sight of Arliss being down, the vampire near Beau rushed at him.

While the two of them began exchanging blows, the vampire holding Bradley began to drag her toward a car.

Bradley kicked and struggled against him. Somehow, she knew that if he got her into that car, she was dead. They would torture her to find out what they wanted, and then they would kill her. She wasn't stopping him with her resistance, though. He was too big, too strong.

"Beau!" she screamed in horror. She twisted violently in her assailant's arms, trying to loosen his grip on her. "Beau!" She pushed her feet off the ground, kicking them wildly in the air and forcing all of her weight onto the vampire. She knocked him off balance, nearly dragging him to the ground with the sudden movement.

"Quit struggling!" he snarled.

He had her nearly to the car when, in a last ditch effort, Bradley threw her head back, hitting him in the face. She felt fangs sink into the back of her head, stinging her flesh, but at least he dropped her. Breathing raggedly from the effort used to get free, Bradley started to crawl in Beau's direction.

She didn't even make it a few feet before the vampire grabbed a fistful of her hair. She was pulled backwards, her butt hitting the pavement.

Still clutching her hair, the vampire began to drag her toward the car behind him.

Bradley grabbed his wrist, trying to pull herself free while her feet scrambled and kicked at the pavement. To her horror, she saw Beau take a two-by-four to the gut and double over.

The vampire fighting Beau loomed over him, his weapon raised for another blow.

That was the last thing Bradley saw before she was hauled from the ground and tossed into a trunk.

Her back hit the floor, and the air rushed out of her in a whoosh. It took a moment before she was able to breathe again. She was too stunned and preoccupied with the effort of simply sucking air into her lungs that she couldn't even fight to get free.

Just as the vampire was about to close the trunk on her, there was a sickening thud, and then his body disintegrated into dust.

Eyes wide, Bradley found herself staring up at Beau's concerned face.

"Let's get you out of there," he said gently. Grabbing her arm, he helped her climb out of the trunk and get back onto the ground of the parking lot.

Bradley's legs were trembling in fatigue and terror. They buckled underneath her as adrenaline wore off, and she sunk to the bumper of the car.

She was still trying to collect herself when Beau said, "Sun's rising. We have to get out of here."

Bradley pushed her hair away from her face with shaky fingers. "Don't you have a room booked here? We could...I could help you get inside."

Beau shook his head. "No. If I go into the hotel dripping blood all over the carpet, the manager is going to be suspicious, and in the morning when they find two bodies in the parking lot, they'll come straight for me. Also, Kelvin knows I was here. He'll take that right back to Jordan Craven. It's too risky." He gave her a questioning look. "What about your place?" He glanced nervously at the pink sky, then grimaced.

"My place is fine," Bradley assured quickly. "I don't have a roommate, but..." She bit her lip in apprehension. "It will take at least ten minutes to get there. The sun will be out full blast by that point."

"We'll be fine." Beau walked over to her car and opened the driver's side door. He searched the interior for a moment, then pressed the button to pop the trunk when he found it on the side of the door. "When we get there, pull up to the door. I'll run in and you can meet me inside once you park the car."

Bradley's eyebrows rose as he swung a foot into the trunk. "You're going to ride in there?"

Beau climbed fully inside, folding his long legs up to curl himself in a ball. "Yes. It will keep out the sun."

"You'll suffocate."

"I don't need to breathe." He began to pull the lid of the trunk shut. "I'll be fine. Don't worry. Just get us there, okay?" Without waiting for an answer, he shut himself in.

Giving the car an uneasy look, Bradley gingerly lowered herself into the driver's seat. Her life had become completely insane. She had a vampire in the trunk of her car. She'd just been attacked by a group of supernatural beings. At this moment, she didn't think her life could get any more complicated. "Famous last words, right?" she asked under her breath.

Chapter 10

Bradley sat on her bed pretending to read a book. She wouldn't have been able to concentrate even if her life depended on it. Her entire world had just been flipped upside down. Vampires existed. At this very moment, there was one in her small, off campus apartment with her. There was a vampire in her shower! She counted to ten, trying to keep herself from hyperventilating. There was a vampire in her shower. So what? It was only Beau.

Nervously, she glanced into the hallway. She'd left her bedroom door open and all the lights on in the hall. The bathroom was across the hallway, so she'd see Beau when he came out.

She was at a loss of what to say to him. How should she react? Should she be afraid of him? He was a vampire, after all, but he'd saved her life. He was a good vampire...right?

The bathroom door opened and Bradley scrambled to her feet. Before she could even think about what she wanted to say, Beau was in the doorway to her bedroom.

He stood there in nothing but a towel. He was a big man, so the towel barely made it halfway down his muscular thighs. A drop of water trailed down his chest, then over his muscled stomach to disappear into the towel. His hair was slicked back from his forehead. It brushed along the back of his neck, dripping beads of water onto his shoulders every so often.

The book fell from Bradley's hand and she found it unexpectedly hard to breathe...and why the hell was it so hot all of a sudden? "You're naked," she accused, as if he didn't realize his state of dress...or undress, for that matter.

Beau's lip curved into a wicked grin at her reaction. "I am not. I have on a towel." He leaned against the doorframe and surveyed her casually. "I didn't have anything else to wear. My clothes were in shreds."

Bradley's eyes roamed over the deep, ragged gashes on his broad chest. She took in his swollen lip, his heavy eyelid, horror rising in her once again. It was like being doused with a bucket of cold water as the memory of their battle in the Holiday Inn parking lot came rushing to the surface.

"Do you have anything I can wear?" Beau asked gently, obviously sensing her fear.

"Wear?" Bradley asked, distracted now by his wounds more than his physique. Finally realizing what he was asking, she nodded and moved over to her dresser. Rummaging around in her drawers, she found a pair of sweatpants that she had borrowed from her brother when crashing at his place a couple weekends ago. She handed them to Beau and resumed her search.

"These didn't belong to an old boyfriend, did they?" came Beau's suspicious voice.

Bradley was glad she was facing away from him so he wouldn't see the blush that crept up her cheeks. "No," she mumbled. "Brother." She finally found what she was looking for, a baggy Marvin the Martian t-shirt. It was one of her favorites, actually, and she didn't lend it out lightly, but Beau had saved her life. Spinning to face him, she found herself staring into his chest.

Though clean of blood, it still was full of deep slashes that looked horribly painful.

Bradley raised a hand, about to run her fingers over one of the angry scratches. She caught the action and froze. Part of it was that she was afraid to hurt him, but the biggest reason she hesitated was for the simple fact that she wanted to touch him. That realization scared her, so instead of touching him, she shoved the t-shirt into his hand.

Beau looked down at the shirt with a slight frown of disapproval on his face. "Marvin the Martian? You want a vampire to wear a Marvin the Martian t-shirt?"

The incredulous look on his face put Bradley at ease and had her tension draining away. Vampire or no, he was still Beau. She couldn't help but laugh as she asked, "How does a vampire even know who Marvin the Martian is? If you know him, you're not too good to wear him."

Beau's eyes narrowed, but his grin was playful. "Fine. I'll

wear the shirt."

"You could always spend the day naked," Bradley teased. "If you are going to be all high and mighty over what I give you, then perhaps you should suffer."

Beau turned and started for the bathroom. "Trust me. If I'm spending the day naked with you, there isn't going to be any suffering going on." With that, he closed the bathroom door behind him.

And just like that, Bradley's tension returned. The thought of Beau strolling naked around her apartment made her weak in the knees. She wouldn't survive that. Seeing him in the towel had almost done her in.

She sunk to the bed, trying to calm her pounding heart. She couldn't get the image of Beau's broad shoulders, or his flawless abs, out of her mind. "Calm down," she advised herself. "He's just a guy. He's no different than any other guys you know...except he's a vampire...and unless you count the fact that he's unbelievably sexy...and actually interested in you. Nothing special about that at all."

Bradley bit her lip at that, gnawing on it in concern. She was worried over the thought that Beau might honestly like her. She had an inkling as to why that bothered her so much. It was because deep down she had to admit to herself that she liked him in return.

He was funny and sexy. He had a smile to die for...and dimples. Did she mention he had the most adorable dimples when he smiled? There was also the most damning piece of evidence that something might be happening between the two of them. The look of complete concern on his face when he'd helped her out of that trunk had her heart pattering at just the memory. He had been truly worried about her. He'd tried to hide it, but she'd seen it in his eyes. He cared.

She sat there pondering that for a few minutes, trying to figure out where this whole thing with him was going. She was so lost in her own thoughts that it took her awhile to realize that Beau had been in the bathroom for quite some time. He was only supposed to be changing, so it shouldn't be taking him this long.

Brows furrowed in concern, Bradley tiptoed to the bathroom door and knocked. "Beau?" she whispered. "Are you okay?" There was nothing but silence in return. Frowning, she knocked again, louder this time. "Beau?" She bit her lip and waited a beat. "You're starting to scare me."

Everything was still silent inside the bathroom.

"Beau, I'm coming in," she warned and turned the doorknob. Creeping in, she found him dressed, but he was hunched over the sink with his eyes squeezed tightly shut. "Beau?" Taking a step closer, she could see that his left hand was buried in his hair. He was touching something...

"Get out," Beau ordered, his teeth clenched in pain as he pulled away a wad of bloody toilet paper and tossed it into the wastebasket. His voice wasn't mean, but demanding. He didn't want her to see whatever it was he was doing.

Bradley frowned and took a step closer. Something wasn't right. There was something there besides toilet paper and blood, something white... Taking another tentative step forward, she saw exposed bone glistening in the bathroom light. It took her a moment to comprehend that she was staring at his skull. Part of his skull was showing through his split skin! She gave a yelp of horror and jumped backwards, slamming into the shower door, causing it to rattle in its frame. "Oh shit. Oh shit. Oh shit."

"You weren't supposed to see that," he said calmly.

"I can see your skull!" she shrieked in alarm. "What...how... I need to call you an ambulance." She spun to race out of the room, but Beau's arm reached out and grabbed her wrist.

He pulled her to an abrupt stop. "You don't call an ambulance for a vampire. We heal on our own."

"Your skull is showing!"

He shrugged with indifference. "Wouldn't be the first time."

"Wouldn't be the first time?" Bradley put a hand to her forehead, feeling completely overwhelmed. "I don't understand. You seemed fine five minutes ago."

"I was hiding the pain well." He dabbed more tissue to the wound. "I'd stopped most of the bleeding earlier, but I bumped it when I was getting dressed."

"What did you bump it on, an axe?" Bradley squeaked, voice shrill with disbelief.

Beau sent her a dirty look as he tossed the tissues into the wastebasket. "I hit my arm off of it when I was pulling good old Marvin on."

Bradley caught another glimpse of his skull and felt her

stomach turn. She had to grip the edge of the sink to keep her knees from wobbling. "At least sit down and let me take a look at it," she offered in concern. She knew there wasn't much she could do for him, but if she could see for herself that the bleeding was slowing down, it would make her feel a little calmer. If it wasn't...well, she was a woman. She would think of something. She had to have that nurturing gene somewhere in there.

Beau gave her an insulted look. "I do *not* need someone to care for me." At the innocent, concerned expression she offered, he gave a sigh, relenting. "Fine. If it will make you feel any better to see for yourself that I am perfectly fine, then I will allow you to poke and prod me."

Putting her hands against his back, Bradley guided him into her bedroom. "I'm not going to poke and prod you," she said with a little huff. "I just don't want you bleeding to death on my watch."

Beau couldn't help but grin as she pushed him down to sit on the edge of the bed, standing in front of him to look down at his injury. "Your watch?" he teased. The thought of needing this fragile human to watch over him was laughable. He could live through more physical abuse than she could even imagine, and she was worried about protecting him. It was actually kind of endearing.

Bradley glared down at him. "If it wasn't for me, you'd be nothing more than ash blowing in the wind right now." She took satisfaction in the way his smug smirk fell. "You need my help," she informed him. Nudging his knees apart with one of her own, she stepped between his legs so she could see the top of his head easier. Leaning over him, she gently brushed his hair to the side so she could see his wound.

Beau frowned. "I don't need help." He winced as Bradley touched his tender skin. "I would have been perfectly fine if I would have done my job correctly from the beginning, then gotten out."

Bradley froze, staring down at the exposed bone of his skull, too distracted now to be bothered by it. "What would doing your job have meant for me?" she asked quietly, though she already knew the answer.

"If I'd have been doing my job properly, I would have killed you and been gone already."

"Why didn't you?" she whispered, her voice wavering.

Beau stayed silent, staring at the wall across the room, avoiding even looking at her.

Bradley let out an unsteady breath, shaken by what his silence meant. "Whatever the reason, I'm grateful." Lowering her hand, she ran her thumb over his swollen eyebrow. After a moment's hesitation, she leaned over and tenderly kissed it.

He jumped in surprise, his eyes lifting to hers.

"Feel any better?" she teased, amused by the startled expression on his face.

He let out a low, masculine laugh. "Much." He gave her a crooked grin, dimples appearing in his cheeks. "That's one thing I didn't normally get when working alone. Ashton never kisses my boo-boos when I get home."

Bradley laughed, shaking her head in amusement. "I'd be a little worried if he did."

"*You* would be?" Beau asked with a chuckle. "I think it would worry me a bit more than it would you."

She smiled down at him for a moment before leaning in and kissing his other eyebrow. "Well, I'd better continue to treat you to such things, so you don't change your mind about breaking the rules for me."

"I don't think getting my boo-boos kissed is a fair exchange for having my skull nearly bashed in," Beau joked, his voice light as she kissed the tip of his nose.

Bradley hesitated only a moment before brushing her lips against his.

"That's an acceptable reward," he informed her. He pulled back slightly so he could study her face. "Why do you wait until I'm in so much pain that I can't do anything about it to kiss me?"

"Because it's safer that way," she whispered honestly. Beau's injuries were a good excuse to keep herself in check. His wound kept her from getting too involved. She didn't know if her heart could take falling in love with him. She'd been in a few relationships that had their challenges, but dating a vampire was setting herself up for heartache. There was no good end to that one.

Beau grimaced. "Doesn't feel safer to me," he teased, giving the top of his head a gentle pat as he referred to his injuries.

His comment drew her eyes back to his head wound, to

his puffy, swollen eye. Once again running her thumb over his eyebrow, she pushed her fears to the back of her mind and asked, "If you were to feed, would this heal quicker?" Stereotypically, vampires survived on blood. She didn't think offering him a bowl of chicken noodle soup was going to do the trick. He needed what his body knew how to turn into energy.

Beau looked as if he didn't want to answer, but he finally let out a sigh. "Yeah. I would heal a lot faster."

Bradley leaned down and brushed her lips across his swollen eyelid. "And I'm the only one who can feed you," she breathed against his skin.

"Looks like it," he replied, his voice soft and almost vulnerable

Pulling back, she nervously searched his face. "It doesn't hurt, does it?"

Beau stared up at her, blue eyes full of honesty. "I would never do anything to hurt you."

Using both hands, she brushed his hair back from his forehead where it had fallen forward. "Then drink from me."

Beau's eyebrows rose in surprise. "Drink from you? I thought you didn't believe in all this vampire stuff."

"I didn't," Bradley admitted, "but I saw a man turn to dust today." She gingerly touched Beau's scalp. "I saw you walk away with an injury that would have killed a normal man." She dropped her hand, staring at him with wide, uncertain eyes. "So, yeah. I'm starting to believe." She knew her eyes must be full of fear at the thought of what believing him meant, at the realization that her life was in serious jeopardy by no fault of her own.

"Believing me and offering yourself up as food are two very different things," Beau warned. "Are you sure you're ready for this?"

"You said that you'd never hurt me," she reminded him, sinking to sit beside him on the bed. "If I can believe in the fact that you're a vampire, I can trust that you're telling the truth when you say you won't hurt me."

Beau's lip curled into a soft smile. "I promise. You won't be hurt in the least." He lifted his left hand and placed it on the side of her neck. Using that hand, he drew her toward him.

Bradley couldn't help but tense when he nuzzled into her

neck.

"Relax," he reassured with a laugh. "There's nothing to be afraid of."

"Sorry," she whispered, jumping in surprise when he pressed a kiss to her collarbone. "I've just never been-" She cut off with a gasp as his fangs sunk into her throat. "I've never been food before," she squeaked.

She awaited the pain that should have followed having her skin pierced, but it never came. Instead, a slow, giddy sensation started to roll through her. The giddiness turned into eagerness, which melded into delight. With each draw of blood Beau took, new emotions swept through her. Fear, excitement, need...love.

Bradley closed her eyes and let all these sensations flow through her, each one more intoxicating than the last. "Is it always like this?" she asked, shivering as Beau's tongue lapped at the tiny puncture marks he'd made in her flesh.

"Humans always find feeding sexually arousing," he admitted, sounding guilty at the effect he had on other women he'd fed off of, "but I don't normally play with my food this much." He proved his point by nuzzling his nose along her jaw. "And I don't normally reciprocate the arousal." His fangs slid back into the shallow holes, and he drew more blood to the surface.

"So you're saying this...this is..." Unable to find a better way to put it, Bradley asked, "So this is like getting to second base for you?"

Beau let out a laugh against her throat. "Third, sweetheart," he said playfully. Pulling back, he licked his lips, checking to make sure they were free of blood. He then leaned forward and kissed her.

She melted into his arms, leaning against his chest. Now that she'd finally admitted to herself that she had feelings for Beau, it felt so right to just let go and enjoy... She pulled her mouth from his, eyeing him suspiciously. "But only with me right?"

He gave that adorable, lopsided grin. "Only with you," he confirmed. He moved back toward her, returning to her neck. He carefully slid his fangs back into the marks he'd previously made, being extremely careful not to hurt her.

Bradley gave a sharp intake of breath as he drew another mouthful of blood, sending a pleasurable jolt through her body. Her skin tingled where he ran his hands over her shoulders, sliding them with a feather light touch down her arms. "I never expected this to feel good," she whispered in amazement after he withdrew his fangs once again.

He ran his tongue quickly over the puncture wounds before sitting back with a smile. "I fully expected it to be good." He studied her questioningly, his eyes full of concern. "How are you feeling?"

She ran a hand over her throat, pausing to assess how she felt. "Good...surprisingly." Her eyes caught his and she felt her cheeks flush in embarrassment. Quickly, she averted her gaze. "Perhaps a little dizzy. Kinda lightheaded...a little tired," she admitted.

"I took a lot," Beau admitted. "I'm sorry." Grabbing her shoulders, he guided her to lie back on the bed. "You just need to take it easy for a little bit, get some sleep." He straightened out to lie next to her on his side, propping himself up on his elbow so he could look at her. "I wouldn't normally take so much. I got greedy because I was hurting." Reaching over, he brushed some of her hair away from her face. "Thank you," he said softly. The words felt almost foreign to him. It had been a long time since someone had done something for the sake of his welfare. It felt odd, and surprisingly nice.

"Don't mention it," Bradley mumbled. "I'm willing to help out a friend anytime."

"Friend? So we're friends now?" he asked, voice full of amusement. He found it cute that she had such trouble admitting that she might have romantic feelings for him. What she'd just done for him went beyond what friends would be willing to do for one another, but he would take this simple admittance as a start. "And anytime?" he repeated in delight as the end of her statement sunk in.

Bradley opened one eye and set him with a stern look. "Don't push it, fang boy."

"Fang boy?" Beau cried with a laugh.

"Dracula?" she offered.

"Dracula doesn't exist," he informed her with regret. "Rumor has it he was a prank. Some vampire out there decided to have a laugh at mankind by feeding them a line of bull."

"Oh," she said in disappointment. "That sucks."

"We tend to do that."

She rolled onto her side, snuggling into her pillow. "I had you guys pegged all wrong. You don't seem evil."

"I'm not evil." Beau paused in thought. "At least not completely."

She gave him a soft, tired smile. "You're not scary either."

A look of indignation crossed his face. "I am scary! Horrifying, even."

Bradley giggled and ran her fingertips over his chest. "You are wearing a Marvin the Martian t-shirt. You're decidedly not terrifying."

Beau went to argue until he heard her next statement.

"I find you kind of cute, though. A vampire in that shirt is just too adorable." She gave a little yawn. "And you're nice. You didn't let those men kidnap me." Closing her eyes, she mumbled, "I think I like you."

He smiled at her continued reluctance to admit her feelings. "I like you too, little Bella."

"Don't call me that," she grumbled, sounding on the verge of falling asleep.

"Sorry," Beau said fondly. "I like you too, Bradley."

Her eyes peeked open and she stared at him through bleary, tired eyes. She lifted a hand and ran one of her index fingers gently along his eyebrow. "You're healing," she said in amazement. A feeling of pride rushed through her. "Letting you drink from me worked."

He grabbed her hand and brought it to his lips, kissing her fingertips. "Yes. It did, and I am unbelievably grateful." He lowered her hand to the bed with some reluctance. He wanted to touch her a little longer, wanted to talk with her some more, but knew she needed to recover from the loss of blood. "You need to get some rest. You are going to need to build your strength back up for the problems that still lie ahead of us. Sleep, and I will make sure you are protected."

Bradley felt the last of her tension ease out of her shoulders. She'd been worried that she wouldn't be able to sleep. Being alone after everything she'd just learned was a scary thought. Knowing Beau would be with her made everything less frightening. She felt relieved knowing he wouldn't be leaving her side.

"While you sleep, I will try to think of a resolution to our problems," he assured. "Tomorrow things won't seem so bleak. I promise. I've had people trying to kill me before. I know."

She took comfort in his words. Beau was experienced at this sort of thing. He would find a way to get them out of this. "Thank you." She waited a beat, almost hesitating with her next sentence. "Goodnight," she whispered.

"I fully agree," Beau said, watching protectively over her as she fell asleep.

Chapter 11

Bradley awoke alone with her heart pounding fiercely in her chest. She'd been torn from sleep by a loud crashing noise from the next room. Pulling her blanket tighter around herself, she stared into the near darkness. "Beau?" she whispered with an edge of fear in her voice.

By instinct, she was quiet because deep down she knew the noise in the other room wasn't Beau bumping into something in the dark. It was an intentional sounding crash, like something being thrown to the ground. Someone was trashing her apartment. Her eyes flicked to the clock on her nightstand. Ten-thirty. Plenty late enough for vampires to be on the move. She would place her bets on whoever was in the other room being associated with the men who had attacked her and Beau in the Holiday Inn parking lot.

There was another loud bang, and then the sound of glass shattering.

The mental image of her mahogany and glass coffee table being overturned filled her mind, and Bradley gave a yelp of fear that she attempted to stifle with her hand. She wanted to call out for Beau again, but was afraid to draw the attention of the person in the next room.

As silently as possible, she climbed to her feet and searched the room for something that could be used as a weapon should the person come after her. Her eyes came across stuffed animals, clothing, a stack of romance novels, beauty accessories. "Why do I have to be so girly?" she mouthed silently, rolling her eyes in frustration.

Then she remembered the baseball bat in her closet. It had been a Christmas gift from Camden the year they started college. He'd reasoned that she could fight off zombies or robbers, whichever she happened to come across first. She'd shoved the bat to the back of her closet and chocked it up to Camden being...well, Camden. It was scary how close to the truth he'd come. She wasn't facing any zombies, but she was fending off homicidal vampires.

She riffled around in the closet, tossing shoes out of her way. While she searched, she kept an ear on what was going on in the other room, not wanting to be caught by surprise any more than she had to be. It sounded like there was a group of strangers in there, and they weren't here to socialize. She had a feeling they were here to find her grandmother's necklace. Killing whomever they ran into was probably somewhere high on their list, as well.

Finally locating the bat, Bradley tiptoed over to the door and raised her weapon above her head, preparing to pummel whoever came into the room. She didn't have to wait long before the door was suddenly kicked in. Wood splintered as the door broke off its hinges, sending small shards flying through the air as it fell to the ground with a loud thump.

A large man stepped through the gaping hole where the door had been. He was tall with dark, cocoa-colored skin and his eyes glowed silver with otherworldly power.

As he entered the room, Bradley brought the bat down as roughly as she could. The force of the blow sent tremors up both of her arms, but the grunt from the man as he collapsed to the floor made the pain worth it.

The man hit the ground, his mouth gaping open and eyes rolling back into his head. He stayed down, unconscious on her bedroom floor.

"Holy crap," Bradley breathed in disbelief. She didn't have much time to linger on this success because another man stepped through the door.

Once inside the room, the man skidded to a halt in surprise. "Donovan's down!" he hollered to the other men in the living room.

Bradley used the second in which he was distracted to swing the bat into the side of his head.

The man stumbled into the sliding door of the closet and struggled to stay upright as his momentum knocked it off its track.

Bradley barely had enough time to bring the bat back around before a third man was in the doorway.

When she swung the bat in his direction, he caught it

with his hand and yanked it from her grasp. "Nice try." He tossed the bat behind him into the living room where it skidded with a clatter across the floor.

Bradley listened to her only hope of defending herself slide out of her reach. Acting on impulse, she raced around the side of her bed to her phone and frantically began punching in Camden's number. She was barely halfway through when the phone was slapped from her hand.

It flew into the wall and smashed into pieces, falling uselessly to the ground.

The next instant she was being tossed facedown onto the bed.

The man that had taken her bat climbed onto the bed after her and pressed a knee roughly into her lower back. He yanked one of her arms behind her back, pinning her to the mattress. Leaning down, he whispered in her ear, "You'd better pray I kill you quick."

Bradley struggled underneath him, but the man only applied more pressure to her spine. "Stop struggling," he threatened, "or I'll break your arm."

From the doorway came a cruel, menacing laugh. "Lookie what Kelvin found, guys. A pretty piece of meat."

Grabbing a fistful of Bradley's hair with his free hand, Kelvin yanked her head back. "Where's the artifact?"

"I don't know what you're talking about," she lied, her words trembling with fear.

"You're lying," Kelvin spat in disgust. Looking over his shoulder into the living room, he called out, "Trash the place!"

Malicious laughter filtered in from the other room, chilling Bradley to the bone.

Turning his attention back to the woman underneath him, Kelvin's voice lowered so only Bradley could hear it, intimidation coming off of him in waves. "Do you know what happens to people who lie to me?" He didn't even give her a chance to respond before he was forcing her face down into one of the pillows. He put his hand at the base of her skull, applying pressure and cutting off her oxygen supply.

Bradley fought against him, but couldn't move enough to jar him off of her. The harder she struggled, the more intense the pain was that shot up her twisted arm.

"The fact that you're Beau's bitch makes this that much

better," Kelvin hissed in her ear as he let go of her head.

Bradley sucked a big mouthful of air into her burning lungs. "Stop," she sobbed hoarsely. "Please stop."

"Then tell me where the artifact is," Kelvin demanded, jamming his knee into her spine to send agonizing pain shooting through her back.

In that instant, Bradley truly believed with all her heart that everything Beau had told her was the truth. If this man got a hold of her grandmother's necklace, he would use it to destroy hundreds of people's lives. No matter what, she couldn't hand it over to him. "I don't have it," she sobbed into the pillow.

Kelvin rolled her violently to her back and straddled her waist, jarring her aching arm as he flipped her. "Don't lie to me! You have it! I know you do!"

"I don't," she sobbed. "I don't."

Kelvin's hands circled her throat and he squeezed down on her windpipe. "We will find it!" he screamed down at her.

A strangled gargle escaped Bradley's throat and stars danced before her eyes. Her vision swam and the terrifying knowledge that this man was going to kill her overwhelmed her. She clawed at Kelvin's hands, desperately trying to kick him off of her. Even through her blurred vision, Bradley saw one of Kelvin's men go flying through the air past the doorway. A moment later, a thud sounded as he hit a wall. She'd barely been able to see it around Kelvin's shoulder, but the sound of the impact made it sound like it had really hurt.

The man hit the ground just outside the door with a grunt of pain at the force with which he'd been tossed.

"We've got company!" one of the men yelled, concern rising in his voice.

Kelvin released her neck and sat back, cursing under his breath. He then rolled off the bed and disappeared from sight.

Bradley wheezed, air rushing into her lungs in a painful burst. She coughed and rolled onto her side as nausea swept over her. It took her a moment to regain her wits and fight back the urge to vomit. Choking and gagging, she somehow managed to get off the bed and climb to her feet, though her legs trembled in protest. She stumbled and fell to her knees, coughing sporadically.

Gripping the edge of the bed, she forced herself to a

standing position. Her vision swam for a moment, but the black spots slowly faded away. She noticed that Donovan was no longer on the floor in the doorway. He must have left while Kelvin was choking her. Well, good riddance. She wasn't going to miss seeing him hanging around. Staggering to the doorway, she leaned against the frame for support, staring into her living room.

Beau was in the center of the room engaged in a fight with another vampire. He growled, showing off a vicious set of fangs as he delivered a fist to the jaw of his adversary. His other arm swung around in a fluid motion and jammed a piece of her broken coffee table through the other man's chest.

The man turned to dust, the fragments of his body sprinkling into her carpet.

Bradley felt relief rush through her at the sight of Beau. When the men had stormed her bedroom, she'd been afraid that they'd killed him. She'd also had the horrifying thought that maybe her vampire savior had abandoned her. Seeing him fighting the bad guys in her living room nearly brought tears to her eyes. "Beau!" she called out to him, her voice hoarse and thick with emotion.

He spun to look at her and his eyes filled with fury at seeing her tears and reddened throat. With a roar of outrage, he turned to the nearest man and dove on him.

The man had seen the murderous look in Beau's eyes and had been in the process of trying to escape, but Beau dragged him to the ground.

He pummeled the man with his fists, showing no mercy in his rage. "How dare you come here and challenge me!" he hollered.

The man didn't even have time to try to defend himself before Beau drove a piece of wood into his chest.

As the man disintegrated, Beau's eyes lifted, and he looked around the now empty room. "Kelvin split," he growled, finally looking to her.

Bradley didn't even look to her jewelry box as she spoke. She'd seen the truth when she'd stumbled past her dresser. "He took my grandmother's necklace." She looked pleadingly at Beau, praying he wouldn't be mad at her. "I didn't tell him where it was. I swear."

Cursing under his breath, Beau turned and raced off into

the night.

Bradley watched him go, her legs shaking in fear. Taking a small, unsteady step forward, she entered the living room and surveyed the damage. Tables had been broken, her couch was overturned, and the television screen had been shattered when it was thrown to the floor.

With trembling hands, she bent down and picked up a framed picture of herself and Camden that had been knocked to the ground. She'd never felt so violated in her life. These people had trashed her home, had looted through her belongings.

To keep herself from bursting into tears, she picked up the living room's cordless phone from the floor and dialed Camden's number. Talking to him would be a distraction. Hopefully it would be enough to keep her from having a total breakdown.

When Camden answered, Bradley calmly told him of the events that had gone on over the past few hours. She ignored his questions of concern, keeping her mind trained on the simple facts and not the emotions that went with them. If she took time to think about the horrible things that had been done to her, she would start crying and she didn't want that. She told him everything as if she was an outsider and not the person that had just nearly been choked to death. If she pretended it wasn't her, she wouldn't have to deal with the emotional baggage that went along with nearly being murdered.

As she was telling Camden why they were late in meeting him, a sound in the doorway drew her attention. She looked up to see Beau stagger back into the apartment looking winded. "I have to go," she said, hanging up the phone and dropping it absentmindedly to the floor, her attention on the vampire in front of her.

"I lost them," Beau wheezed out. "They got into a car. I'm fast, but I can't outrun a Toyota."

Bradley stared at him for a moment in perplexity. She was fascinated by his winded state. Vampires supposedly didn't breathe. How could they get winded? She went to ask him about this, but instead, what came out was, "Where were you?" Her own question caught her off guard, surprising her with the amount of vulnerability in her voice.

Beau's eyes filled with guilt. "I ran across the street to

the grocery store for juice."

She blinked in surprise. "You left for juice? That's not at all random."

His lip quirked in a half smirk and he shrugged. With a nod to the carton of orange juice on the counter, he said, "Feeding a vampire takes a lot out of a person. It's the same concept as donating blood to a hospital. You need sugar and the like to keep from getting dizzy."

"Sugar?"

"I bought donuts too," Beau offered helpfully. "I wasn't sure what kind you liked, so I bought two dozen."

Bradley's eyes slid to the two boxes on the counter that held the donuts. They looked as if they'd been thrown there haphazardly, as if tossed by someone on the run. Apparently the moment he saw her apartment was being ransacked, Beau had jumped into immediate action, wanting only to keep her safe. "That has to be the most romantic thing anyone's ever done for me," she whispered.

Their eyes met and Beau started toward her.

Bradley met him halfway and fell into his arms, leaning against his chest to support her quivering legs.

His mouth was on hers an instant later.

This time, Bradley didn't even hesitate. She wrapped her arms around his waist and leaned in against his strong chest, letting him kiss away her fears.

Beau pulled back long enough to mumble, "You've had some really crappy boyfriends."

She laughed, but his mouth swallowed up the sound.

He kissed her with a desperate urgency. His palms ran down her back, caressing her through her shirt. As his lips kissed along her throat, his feet guided them toward the bedroom.

Bradley let him walk her backwards to the bed. Her hands slid up his chest, over his shoulders, and wrapped around his neck as his mouth moved back to hers.

They tumbled to the bed, their lips never breaking contact.

When they hit the bed, Bradley realized she was still clutching the picture of Camden. She put a hand to Beau's chest and forced him back. When he moved away from her, she noticed her breathing was coming out in breathless pants.

"One second," she promised, leaning in to give him another kiss. That kiss seemed to go on and on, though it was meant to be quick. She wasn't even going to be leaving the room, but the thought of moving out of Beau's comforting embrace seemed abysmal. Finally, she put a hand to his chest and pushed him back once again. "Give me some space, you horny vampire."

"Horny vampire?" Beau chuckled as he sat back on his knees to give her room to sit up.

Bradley giggled at the mock look of indignation on his face. Leaning over to the nightstand, she set down the photo of Camden, straightening it. The rest of her apartment was torn up. At least something would look nice.

Sliding back over to Beau, she gave him a timid smile. "Okay. I'm back." Placing a hand on his cheek, she leaned closer to eliminate the distance between them. She kissed him tenderly, tentative in her inexperience with the emotions flowing through her.

Beau deepened the kiss, wanting to show her how worried he'd been about her. While he poured his emotions into their kiss, he lowered her backwards to the pillow.

Bradley's heart beat furiously at the intensity with which Beau kissed her. She knew he had to hear it, had to feel it against his chest.

He suddenly broke away from her with an agitated snort. Reaching toward the nightstand, he slammed the picture of Camden facedown. Rolling back over, he put himself on top of Bradley, resting between her legs. "That's better."

She giggled, running her fingertips along his jaw. "Afraid Camden will affect your performance?"

Beau grinned down at her, noting the demure way she let him know that she would sleep with him. Her coy, shy attitude was such a breath of fresh air. He'd never been more turned on by a woman in his entire, extremely long life. "I don't like the thought of Camden watching us. No."

He kissed her again, and Bradley gave a startled gasp into his mouth when she felt the hard press of his fangs against her lip.

She waited for him to bite her, was expecting it. After a few moments, she realized that drawing blood wasn't Beau's intention. The elongated state of his teeth was just a natural reaction to what they were doing.

She relaxed further into the kiss, yielding to the silent demand his body was giving. Cautiously, she flicked her tongue out along one of his fangs, exploring something completely foreign to her.

This man had fangs! Real, bona fide, honest to goodness fangs! Beau *was* a vampire. He wasn't some Goth kid playing dress up. He was the real deal.

Amazed by that fact, she once again danced her tongue along the sharpened points of his eyeteeth.

Beau gave a low, pleased moan. His hands balled into fists, and he clutched the sheets between his fingers. "A girl who knows what to do with a set of fangs. I think I've died and gone to heaven," he mumbled against her lips. He moved from her mouth to her neck, nuzzling and caressing along her skin. With bold confidence, he grabbed her shirt in both hands and lifted it over her head. He then tossed it over his shoulder to the floor.

Bradley was glad someone in the room knew what they were doing, because she surely didn't. She'd gotten lucky with her guess about his fangs. She knew as much about vampires as she knew about men, pretty much nothing. Trying to drive that insecurity from her mind, she forced herself to relax. She silently ordered herself to calm down and simply relish Beau taking charge of the situation.

Squeezing her eyes shut, she concentrated on every touch, every movement Beau made. She relinquished all control to him, enjoying the way his fingers trailed sensually along her skin. She knew she shouldn't be doing this, that she should be asking Beau to leave. She barely knew him...but she didn't want him to stop. God. It felt so good to be wrapped up in his protective embrace.

He was so tender and gentle with her. He was treating her with a delicacy that made her feel treasured. He made her feel like no one ever had before in her life.

As he slid her jeans over her thighs, Beau kissed an exceptionally sensitive spot on one of her hips and all thoughts of anything else flew from her mind. She suddenly didn't care how bad of an idea this was. She wanted it anyway, wanted him.

Biting her lower lip, Bradley tried to keep from squirming when the attention that was being lavished on her tickled. Though she wriggled, she was fully relaxed for the first time in as long as she could remember.

Beau set about removing the rest of her clothing; his hands moved with skill along her body even though the room was dark. He moved swiftly, giving in to his frantic, primal urges.

He didn't know why, but he needed her. He needed her right now. There was almost a desperation about the way he needed to feel the touch of her skin against his own. He'd survived a long time without a woman in his life, but he suddenly couldn't fathom his future existence without Bradley. He couldn't wait another ten minutes to be with her.

Though he began stripping his own clothing at a brisk pace, Beau kept his senses cautiously attuned to Bradley, searching for even the slightest hint of reluctance. When he found none, he tossed the last piece of fabric separating them to the floor.

He found that patience was something he had little of as he lowered his body to hers, reveling in the feel of her silky skin against him. Without warning, he slid himself inside of her, giving a low groan at the sensation of their joining.

Bradley gave a sharp, shaky gasp, her fingers gripping tightly to his shoulder blades. "Beau," she whispered into his neck, burying her face into the comforting feel of his skin.

He lowered his head and captured her mouth with his as, with each thrust, he plunged deeper and deeper into her. "Bradley," he breathed against her mouth, his voice gravelly with emotion.

She gave another gasp of delight as he brushed a thumb along one of her nipples, tightening it instantly. "Bella," she managed to get out between their frantic kissing. "Call me Bella."

Beau chuckled, the sound as manly as anything she'd ever heard. "Mmm, Bella. My little Bella." His tongue ventured into her mouth, brushing against her teeth.

An idea entered Bradley's mind and, before she could even think it through, she ran her tongue along the sharp point of one of his fangs.

The fang scratched along her tongue, causing little droplets of blood to spring to the surface.

She moved her tongue back to his, letting her blood tease along his taste buds.

Beau gave a sound of surprise at the sweet tang of a

taste that was all Bradley. The shock of it threw him into orgasm long before he'd intended to let himself. He gripped Bradley's hips and drove into her one last time while her blood flooded his senses with pleasure.

His body trembling and emptying inside of her pulled Bradley into ecstasy along with him. Wave after wave of pleasure danced through her body. She had no choice but to cling to Beau and ride out the spine-tingling sensations.

A moment later, Beau collapsed half on top of her. "You...you shouldn't have done that," he wheezed into her shoulder.

"Why not?" Bradley asked in concern, worried that she'd done something wrong.

"I was trying to last a little longer than five minutes," he grumbled, not sounding too overly upset about their encounter.

Bradley smiled, her expression one of giddy joy. "I thought it was perfect. Your reaction let me know that I actually did something right."

He nodded, his hair tickling her ear. "Did you ever."

She closed her eyes, letting his body heat sink into her skin. She felt tired and lazy...and happier than she'd ever been in her entire life. It didn't matter that her apartment was trashed or that people were trying to kill her. What mattered was the way Beau made her feel.

She was having some seriously strong feelings for him and that scared her. She wasn't used to the emotions that were flowing inside of her. Trying to push the fear of having him break her heart to the back of her mind, she instead concentrated on how safe she felt in his arms. With that thought in mind, she began drifting into a light, peaceful sleep because she knew Beau was watching over her, and he would do everything in his power to keep her safe.

Chapter 12

Beau lay in bed just listening to Bradley's slow, even breathing. With his ear against her shoulder, he could hear the steady beat of her heart. That sound nearly brought tears to his eyes. The last time he'd been this emotionally close to a living human...well, he almost couldn't remember.

It felt so good holding Bradley in his arms, having her tiny body tucked possessively against him, that he never wanted to let her go. He could lay here for hours and still not want to get up. He didn't have the luxury of doing that, though. The twenty minutes he'd let Bradley sleep while he organized his thoughts was probably longer than he should have allowed. Craven's men had Bradley's necklace, and he needed to get it back. He'd decided his first step of action would be to call Ashton in for help. Beau knew he could trust him to keep Bradley safe.

Ashton was better at sympathizing with humans. He would be helpful in this situation because he cared more about people's welfare than anyone Beau knew. He would do everything in his power to resolve their issue without anyone getting hurt.

They also had Camden waiting for them. Beau didn't want to leave him alone for much longer. He didn't want any-thing bad to happen to Camden. Beau would never forgive himself if something were to happen because he greedily wanted to lie in bed with Bradley a little longer.

Cupping Bradley's right cheek in his hand, Beau pressed a kiss to the opposite ear. "We need to get moving," he whispered into her hair. Rolling over, he slid out of bed and strode to the bedroom doorway. "Camden is waiting for us." He leaned against the doorframe, gazing at her with affec-tion. "Get up, cutie," Beau said with a slight grin at her mussed hair.

Bradley gave a sleepy murmur at being roused after only a twenty minute nap. "Tell Camden to drive here himself," she grumbled halfheartedly.

"He can't," Beau informed her with a fond grin. "I have his car." The memory of Camden accusing him of wanting to keep the car filled his mind. "Shit," he mumbled to himself, giving a chuckle of amusement. "He's going to think I actually did steal his car."

Still laughing, Beau turned and meandered into the bathroom. He began to prepare for the full day he knew he had ahead of him. He moved quickly, finishing in a record four minutes, his haste due to his impatience to get to Camden's.

Strolling back to the bedroom, Beau found Bradley standing in front of the mirror, staring at her still naked body. His eyebrows rose in question as he pulled on the sweatpants she'd given him the night before. "You okay there?"

Bradley turned to the side, eyeing herself critically. "Yeah, I was just..." She shrugged. "I know it's silly, but I expected to look a little different, I guess."

"Look different?" Beau asked in amusement as he pulled the Marvin the Martian t-shirt over his head. "Why would you look different? Having sex with a vampire is just the same as a human man. We all have the same parts." He gave her a crooked grin as he tugged the shirt down over his chest and stomach. "You sound like someone who's never..." He trailed off in horror, his eyes widening in realization and his hands freezing in their movements. "Were you a virgin?"

Bradley blushed and looked down at her hands so she wouldn't have to look into his eyes.

Her lack of an answer told him all he needed to know. "Why didn't you tell me?" he asked in shock.

"Because it wasn't a big deal," she mumbled in embarrassment.

"Not a big deal?" Beau cried in disbelief. "For your first time...I would have been gentler. I could have hurt you!" Fear filled him at the thought that he may have done exactly that. "Did I hurt you?"

"No!" Bradley cried in reassurance. "It was perfect."

A smug look flitted across Beau's face, but he quickly fought for neutrality.

"This conversation is exactly why I didn't tell you. You

would have treated me differently. You already act as if I'm made of glass because I'm human." She let out a sigh and her hands dropped to her sides. "Listen. I never slept with anyone else before because it had never been about me. The guys I've dated were only looking to fulfill their own sexual needs. I was replaceable in their scenario. As long as they were getting what they wanted, it didn't matter who was with them." With a little shrug, she said, "When we...it was about me. You cared about what had happened to me. You were worried. I saw it in your eyes. You were upset because I was hurt."

"I was," Beau agreed, his voice low and husky with emotion.

"That's why I did it. Because you wanted *me*," Bradley said. "I didn't tell you because...well, I'm not an idiot. I don't expect you to..." She looked up into his blue eyes. "You're a vampire. You were probably alive before my grandfather was born. I don't see you in a relationship and that's okay. I'm just glad, at that point and time, I meant something to you."

"That point and time?" Beau asked, a little sharply. He moved in closer until the front of his shirt brushed against her bare flesh. "I haven't had sex in sixty-five years. This wasn't just a whim decision. Don't make it seem like it was just a heat of the moment thing. I've wanted you from the moment I laid eyes on you. Just because I'm a vampire doesn't mean I'm incapable of feeling."

Bradley's eyes had widened to the size of saucers at how long he'd been abstinent. "I...I..." She turned away from him as if looking into his eyes was too much. "If I let myself fall for you, I just know it will be hard. I'll be that stupid, clingy, needy girl that drives men away and it will break my heart when you leave. That's not something I want to do to myself." Trying to keep him from seeing the tears that sparkled in her eyes, she attempted to push past him. In her heart, she knew that it might be too late to keep herself from falling for Beau. He had already wormed his way into her heart, and she didn't know if he could easily be forgotten.

Beau grabbed her wrist and pulled her toward him, holding her firm against his chest. "I'm never going to leave you," he said, voice thick with emotion. His mouth was close enough to hers that, when he spoke, their lips brushed together. "I want you to be needy. I want to fill your thoughts every waking moment." His arms slid around her back, caressing her bare skin. "When you go to visit your parents during the day, I want you to be short of breath knowing that when you get home to me, I'm going to ravish you. I want you to fall for me, Bradley."

Bradley's eyes were closed and her pulse quickened. "Do you really mean that?"

"I've been alive over four hundred years and no one has been able to affect me the way you do. I never want that to stop."

"I don't want it to stop either."

He gave her a soft, gentle kiss. "Good. Then it's settled. You are to become madly in love with me and pine for me whenever I am not able to be at your side."

She laughed, shaking her head in amusement. "And what will you be doing while I do all this pining?"

"Killing any man that dares even look in your direction," Beau said as if this was a rational idea.

"Mmm..." she mumbled, standing on tiptoes to brush her lips along his. "My hero." Seeing as she'd witnessed Beau kill half a dozen men in the past twenty-four hours, she found it necessary to add, "Please don't actually kill anyone, though."

He gave a huff as if she was asking too much of him. Leaning down, he gave her another quick kiss. "I promise not to kill anyone unless they really deserve it." He kissed her again before releasing her. "Now go get cleaned up and pack a bag with enough essentials to last you a week. I don't know if it will be safe to come back here once Craven's men have had time to regroup."

Bradley bobbed her head in agreement. "Where will we go after that?"

"First, we'll go pick up Camden. After that point, we're winging it."

Bradley didn't like the idea of winging a life or death situation, but she felt much safer with Beau in charge. She knew he'd do anything in his power to protect her and Camden. She only had to hope that would be enough to keep them alive.

Chapter 13

"This is an outrage," Beau cried in indignation. "I didn't realize when I agreed to protect the two of you that I would be asked to commit such unspeakable acts."

"Oh my goodness!" Bradley came back in disbelief. "You're shopping at Wal-Mart, not selling your soul."

"You're right," he griped. "You usually get something in return for your soul. At least selling my soul might have a few benefits."

"I'm sorry that the Prada Palace isn't open at midnight," she snapped in agitation.

"Prada Palace?" he asked scornfully. "I don't even know what that means."

"I don't know what the people of Prada like to call their stuck up little stores!" She took a deep, calming breath. Yelling at him wasn't going to convince Beau that he was a snob. It would only agitate him further. "What I'm trying to say is that, with the hours you keep, no designer store is open right now. You will have to settle for Wal-Mart, or go naked for the next couple of days." Her voice was haughty, pride filling her as she gave Beau his unappealing ultimatum...only she didn't foresee that he would find the thought alluring.

Beau gave her a steamy, suggestive look that had her blushing down to her toes.

"So you'd better just get over it," she said in conclusion, her voice thick with embarrassment.

Beau had kept a duffle bag of personal belongings in the room he'd had at the Holiday Inn. When Craven's men found where he was staying, they'd taken everything in hopes of finding the necklace, or information on its whereabouts. Beau discovered this when he'd called the hotel about picking up his things. They'd informed him that a Mr. Beauregard Channing had checked out and taken all of his belongings with him. Obviously, this hadn't been the real Beau, but it was impossible to convince the hotel manager of this fact. Now all he had were the clothes on his back, which actually belonged to Bradley. Lucky for him, he'd at least had his wallet with him when he was attacked in the parking lot. He could buy new things, if only he would get off his high horse and just pick something already.

"If you would have told me a week ago that vampires were so prissy, I never would have believed you," Camden said thoughtfully as he perused a rack of shirts. "How about this?" he asked, holding up a t-shirt that read, *I think your girlfriend's fat.*

Beau arched an annoyed eyebrow. "As charming as that is, I will have to pass."

"Really?" Camden gave a frown of disappointment. "I thought that would really get to the bad guys. You know, hit 'em where it hurts."

"That would be the groin!" Bradley called from two racks over.

"Lovely," Beau said sarcastically. Rolling his eyes, he lifted a suit jacket and eyed it in disdain, distracted by the appalling corduroy. "The thought of wearing something that isn't Armani chills me to the bone."

It was Bradley and Camden's turn to roll their eyes. They did so at each other with matching grins.

Beau glared at them and would have commented, but Bradley let out a delighted squeal.

"Beau, look at this!" she cooed. "This is too adorable."

"I am not wearing anything that can be described as 'too adorable'," he griped.

She proudly held up a shirt she'd grabbed from the Halloween section. It was a black t-shirt showing a cartoon vampire in furry slippers and a purple bathrobe holding a steaming cup of blood. Underneath the vampire's feet, it said, *Not a morning person.*

"Absolutely not!" Beau cried.

She gave him a pout. "Why not? Aren't you thrilled that modern culture has been able to capture the fuzzy side of vampires?"

He stared at her pouting bottom lip, momentarily distracted by the urge to nibble on it until he drew a few tiny drops of blood. He blinked, taking that moment to collect himself. "We do not have a fuzzy side."

Camden snorted, and on Bradley's glare, meandered away.

Bradley pouted and waggled the shirt around as if that would change Beau's mind.

Beau's eyes narrowed. "No."

She stamped her foot in agitation. "But it's cute!"

He watched her lips as they drew into a full pout. It was just too tempting to ignore. Wrapping an arm around her waist, he pulled her close and brushed his lips against that tantalizing mouth. "You may be sexy as hell," he breathed, "but I'm not wearing that shirt. Ever." He paused thought-fully. "I'll buy it for you, though, if you promise to wear noth-ing but that to bed tonight."

Bradley pushed on his chest and took a step back, glanc-ing in Camden's direction to see if he'd witnessed their kiss. Luckily, he was distracted. She didn't want him teasing her relentlessly, which she knew he would do if he realized she and Beau were...whatever they were. She tucked a lock of hair behind her ear, giving Beau a sly, embarrassed smile.

Then his statement reminded her of their housing situa-tion. Her grin turned into a confused frown. "Where *are* we going to stay tonight? We can't go back to my place and your hotel is out." With uncertainty, she added, "I would assume we can't stay at Camden's either."

Beau nodded in affirmation. "Though I doubt they know who Camden is yet, they will. Craven doesn't like to leave witnesses, and he surely doesn't like ones who align them-selves with me. He's going to send goons after you again. If they don't find you, they'll track down your friends. It won't be long before they're searching for Camden as well."

"So what are we going to do?" Bradley asked in fear. She was suddenly filled with concern for her friends and family.

"I booked a couple motel rooms for us outside of town. I figured we'd lay low for a while. I can call Ashton and have him help me track down Craven. Then I'll go after him."

"By yourself?" she asked with a gasp.

He nodded. "That's how it usually works."

Her eyes searched his in apprehension. "But that's dan-gerous."

"I find it adorable that you're concerned for my welfare,"

Beau said with a crooked grin, "but this is my job. It's what I do. I'll be perfectly fine."

Worry filled her and she opened her mouth to argue, but Camden interrupted her.

"How about this?" Camden was holding up a t-shirt that said, *Your girlfriend thinks I'm hotter than you*. He had a proud smile on his face at what he considered an ingenious find.

Beau's expression became one of disbelief. "No," he said with feeling. "What is it with you and the girlfriend shirts?"

Camden shrugged. "They're funny, while at the same time, insulting to the bad guys."

"No," Beau repeated firmly. Instead, he grabbed a few button up dress shirts.

"Fine," Camden retorted, sullen. "Be that way." He hung the shirt over his arm and patted it with his hand. "I'm getting one, though." On Beau's disinterested shrug, he added, "Who would have ever thought vampires would be no fun?"

"It's common sense that we aren't any fun," Beau drawled.

"Whatever," Camden said with a roll of his eyes as he walked away.

As soon as Camden was out of hearing range, Bradley cleared her throat. When Beau glanced down at her, she handed the vampire t-shirt over to him and quirked a teasing eyebrow. "I don't know," she whispered suggestively. "I've found a few qualities that I would definitely label as fun."

Beau's blue eyes darkened in interest, taking on a smoldering look. "You haven't even begun to see fun."

"Neither have you," she came back. "You've been behaving yourself for sixty-five years. I'm sure there are quite a few things you've missed in those decades."

His gaze held hers, his eyes full of longing. "And you think you're the one to catch me up to date."

She licked her lips, knowing that he could probably hear the ferocious pounding of her heart. "Unless you have any protests."

His gaze slipped lower, his eyes transfixed on the pulse at her neck. "None whatsoever."

Camden took that moment to return. "Whoa," he said in surprise. "You both look completely intense. I'm not interrupting anything am I?"

There was an uncomfortable pause before Beau said, "No." His eyes slid to Camden, wary of the kid's next horrific discovery. "What rags have you brought me this time?"

"Rags?" Camden cried in an overdramatic manner. "I have brought you a New York Jets hoodie."

Beau's eyes darkened.

"Come *on!*" Camden practically yelled. "Even vampires aren't that soulless! You *have* to like football."

"I love football, actually," Beau replied. "I simply am not a Jets fan."

Bradley tensed and Camden let out a low whistle. "The honeymoon is so over."

Beau looked between the two of them in confusion. "Have I said something wrong?"

Camden sent him an almost pitying look. "Bradley is a huge Jets fan."

"Not a Jets fan?" Bradley shrieked, cutting Camden off from whatever he'd been about to say next. "You're not a Jets fan?" She shook her head in disapproval. "How is that even possible?" Her eyes narrowed in suspicion. "Who *do* you like then?" Horror filled her as she said, "Surely you're not a Patriots fan." Before Beau could even respond, she sucked in a dramatic hiss of air. "Oh my God, you are! You are, aren't you? You're a Patriots fan!"

Beau's face took on a look of disgust at her accusation. "Of course not."

Bradley gave another gasp, her hand flying to her chest and her eyes widening.

"What now?" Beau griped, obviously wondering how he could have possibly done anything else to deserve her wrath.

"The Jets game!" On Beau's puzzled look, she continued. "Every year for the Jets opening game, I go with my brother for his birthday. It's a tradition. I can hide with you until then, but I'm not missing my brother's birthday. The night of the game, I'll have to leave."

Beau crossed his arms over his expansive chest and Bradley knew she was about to have an argument on her hands.

"Until I decide it's safe, you can not go wandering about. It's too dangerous." As if Beau wasn't in enough trouble, he felt the need to add, "I don't allow you."

"Uh-oh," Camden said under his breath.

"You don't allow me?" Bradley asked in angry disbelief. "I wasn't aware I needed your permission." She crossed her arms over her chest in a mimic of Beau's stance, her eyes fiery with frustration. "And to think I was starting to consider you a nice guy." She gave an unladylike snort. "Apparently I was mistaken. You..." She made an irritated noise in the back of her throat. "You are the last man on Earth I would take orders from. You're pushy. You're obnoxious. You're stubborn."

"Oh! *I'm* the stubborn one," Beau cried. "That's funny coming from the Queen of Bullheadedness!"

"People are starting to stare," Camden informed them, a hint of amusement in his voice.

Both Bradley and Beau spun on him with a unanimous, "Shut up!"

Bradley spun back to Beau and poked him in the chest. "You are not my boss and I will do whatever I please, whenever I please."

"It is too dangerous for you to go anywhere without me," Beau came back obstinately.

"Well then I guess you'll just have to go with me then, won't you?" she challenged, her tone heated.

"I guess I will."

"Good."

"Good."

They both stood glaring at each other until Camden broke the silence by asking, "Did you just ask him out on a date?"

Bradley blinked at her friend in surprise. "I...I..." Giving Beau a defiant stare, she said, "Well, I hope you have a miserable time."

"And I hope the Jets lose," Beau came back.

She gave an indignant gasp and pointed an accusing finger in his direction.

Before she could go off on another tirade, Camden grabbed her shoulders and guided her toward the checkout counters. "Let's not argue. We're all stressed out and tired. We're all saying things we don't mean."

"Oh, I mean it," Beau corrected. "I really do hope the Jets lose."

Bradley opened her mouth to argue, but Camden gave her a shove toward the cashier. Spinning on Beau, he hissed, "You're not helping."

Beau gave a lazy shrug. "What can I say? I'm pushy and obnoxious."

"Don't forget arrogant!" she tossed over her shoulder.

Camden shook his head in disbelief. "How are you two going to survive days cooped up together when you can't go on a shopping trip without tearing each other's heads off?"

With a huff, Beau visibly backed down. "It's Wal-Mart. It's evil. It does something to people, turns them into real assholes."

Camden's brows furrowed at Beau's reasoning. "You really have issues. You know that, right?"

Beau gave a little scoff. "Don't I know it," he mumbled, walking toward the checkout counter. "Don't I know it."

Chapter 14

Bradley was lying on the bed of the motel room Beau had checked them into. She and Beau were sharing a room under the guise of a couple on vacation and Camden, "Beau's brother", had gotten the room right next to theirs. Beau had made sure Camden's room had a connecting door to theirs in case anything were to happen. That way they could sneak out the second room if one was attacked.

Bradley would have much rather roomed with Camden, but Beau insisted that she not be out of his sight for a minute. He'd reasoned that Craven's men were after her, not Camden. If they came after anyone, it would be her, and he was making certain he was around to protect her when that time came.

She'd finally agreed to room with him as long as he slept on the small loveseat in the corner of the room. It would be damn uncomfortable for someone of his height, but she sure wasn't sleeping on it.

"I see you're still ignoring me," Beau's agitated voice said from the doorway that separated the bedroom from the bathroom.

Bradley, who was reclining on the bed, looked up from the book in her hand. "I didn't even realize you were out of the shower," she snapped in reply. She gave the book a little shake. "Obviously I was engrossed in something besides your ego. Hard to imagine, right?"

Beau's lip curled back in a snarl.

While he was busy giving her a dirty look, Bradley's gaze traveled to his chest.

He was bare from the waist up, beads of water glistening on his skin.

Damn him. Didn't his mother ever teach him to properly

use a towel? She thought in agitation.

He was wearing a pair of flannel pajama bottoms so low on his hips that it was impossible for him to be wearing anything underneath. Her eyes lifted from the dangerously low waistband to his stomach. She bit her lip, attempting to distract herself from the sight of his abs. They bunched and moved in an absolutely erotic manner, keeping her eyes fixated.

That was when she realized he was doing it on purpose. She looked up to find him leaning against the doorframe, a smug look on his face at the way she was ogling him.

"Why don't you cover up?" she barked in embarrassment, climbing to her feet in an attempt to hide her humiliation. "Not everyone wants to stare at your nipples."

"Perhaps the same could be said for you," he practically growled. His voice wasn't simply angry anymore. It held an almost animalistic desire to it.

Bradley looked down at her top with a mortified gasp. Her wet hair had dripped all over her pajama top, soaking through the fabric. Her breasts could easily be seen through the white fabric, her nipples standing out in dark, hard circles. She pulled the top away from her skin so her assets weren't bared for Beau to see. "That was an accident. You..." She looked up at him accusingly through damp hair. "You did yours on purpose."

Beau stalked his way across the room like a graceful tiger. "I am guilty. Perhaps I do such things because I want you to desire me as much as I crave to touch your silky flesh." His hands grabbed her hips and pulled her toward him, his mouth crushing against hers.

She gave a squawk of protest, but it was halfhearted. Even as she protested, her arms wrapped around his neck to pull him closer.

"I lied to you," Beau confessed. "I do wish to see your nipples. I wish to see them, touch them, and taste them. I wish to nibble on the sensitive buds until you are weak with ecstasy."

Her stomach tightened at his suggestion and she moaned into his mouth. "I lied, as well. I want to see your nipples, too."

"Good," he growled, his mouth demanding against hers. "I could spend the next two hundred years doing nothing but making love to you. You can burn my clothing for all I care. I do not need it." His grip on her hips tightened, pulling her even closer to him.

Bradley felt herself go weak in the knees at the sensation of him against her. Memories of this body and the pleasure it had brought her invaded her mind.

Beau slid his body along hers, rubbing their hips together. This made it perfectly clear that he had nothing on under the thin, flannel pajama bottoms.

She whimpered into his mouth, pressing against him to touch as much of his skin as possible.

His hands moved to her butt as he held her against him, hissing in delight at the sensation of her small, yielding body. One of his hands slid under the t-shirt she wore, forcing it up around her waist. His fingers trailed along her inner thigh until they hit her undergarment. "I thought I told you to wear nothing under this," he chastised.

Bradley didn't even get a chance to comment before his hand slid higher until it cupped her breast in its palm.

He squeezed, rubbing against her nipple, causing a gasp of pleasure to escape her. "I wish to possess you," he growled between kisses, "every night from now to eternity."

"Possess me," she begged into his mouth, her breathing ragged. "Right now. Please, I..."

The door that connected their room to Camden's banged open.

Bradley gave a yelp and jumped away from Beau. Remembering her soaked top, she snatched up her bathrobe and frantically pulled it around herself.

Beau, who had moved away just as guiltily, had sunk down into one of the motel chairs. He swiftly crossed his ankle over his knee and shifted in the chair to best hide his unmistakable arousal.

Camden didn't even notice their discomfort. The distraught look on his face as he paced the room let them know he was too focused on his own problems. "Someone's trying to kill me," he cried dramatically.

Beau cleared his throat and shifted in his seat with a grimace. "Oh yeah?"

Camden spun to face him. "Someone's outside my room," he hissed in a whisper. "I heard someone moving around in the hall, scoping the place out."

This had Beau sitting up in attention. "Are you certain someone's out there?" He slid Bradley a concerned look.

"Positive," Camden assured, his green eyes wide. "They knocked on the door right before I ran in here."

"Attackers don't usually knock," Beau surmised. He climbed gracefully to his feet. "Nevertheless, I will investigate."

Before he could even move, there was a knock at their door.

Camden gave an *"eep"* and jumped behind Beau.

Bradley, always curious, gave him a funny look before walking over to the door. She peered through the peephole, searching the hallway beyond.

"Who is it?" came Camden's frightened voice from behind Beau.

"Bradley, do be careful," Beau advised as he gave Camden a disapproving glance.

Seeing the occupants of the hallway, Bradley gave a huff. "Oh, for goodness sake." Shooting Camden a disbelieving look, she unlocked the door and swung it open.

Beau was at her side in an instant. He shoved her back against the wall as the door swung open, and yelled at the Girl Scouts in the doorway, "State your purpose!" Realizing that two elementary aged girls were staring up at him in wide-eyed horror, he corrected his tone. "What I meant was, what did you need, little girls?" His eyebrows lifted. "Candy? Will that make you go away? You like candy, don't you?"

The girls had backed up a step and their mother gave Beau a wary look.

Bradley pushed off the wall and moved around Beau. "Knock it off," she whispered to him. "You sound like a would-be kidnapper." To the little girls, she said, "I'll take a box of Do-si-dos and a box of Samoas."

"And a box of Thin Mints!" Camden hollered from behind Beau.

"Ew!" Bradley yelled back, but gave the girls a bright smile. "And a box of Thin Mints." Looking back at the room, she absently asked, "Where's my purse?"

"They seek money?" Beau asked in surprise.

"That's usually how this works," Bradley explained as she tossed the boxes of cookies to Camden.

Pulling out his wallet, Beau gave the mother a reproachful look. "I may not be completely up with the times, but I do know that child labor is illegal. You should be ashamed of your actions today," he scolded as he handed a fifty over to one of the girls. Bending down to her height, Beau said, "Keep the change. Hopefully it will keep you from being beaten by your employer when you are through." Patting the girl on the head, he turned and walked away.

Bradley gave the girl's mother a weak smile and waved a hand around her head. "He bumped his noggin earlier today and has been talking crazy ever since. We should really get him checked out. I think he might have lasting brain damage or something."

Before the mother could respond, Bradley rushed on with a nervous titter, addressing the little girl, "Well, all right! Thank you and enjoy that tip. It's not every day a vampire gives you a fifty." Realizing she'd just told the girl that Beau was a vampire, she said, "Damn it! I shouldn't have said that!" Her eyebrows furrowed. "Damn! I shouldn't have sworn in front of little kids... Damn!" she cried, realizing she'd done it again. She clamped her hands over her mouth to keep herself from saying anything else stupid. "I'm sorry about that. Have a nice day," she mumbled unintelligibly into her hands.

The mother's brows tugged down in irritation. "Do I even want to know what you just said?"

Slowly lowering her hands, Bradley said, "Have a nice day." As the group walked away, she felt the need to yell after them. "And I was only kidding about the vampire comment! Haha, right? Funny! And not at all true. Uh-uh. No vampires in *this* motel room," she said, pointing into her room. "You're crazy if you think that!"

They disappeared around a corner in the hallway and Bradley cringed, shutting the door.

Beau sat on the bed, one eyebrow raised in amusement as he wrestled open a box of Do-si-dos. "Those children must have been very skilled in espionage to get you to spill all of our secrets like that."

"Oh shut up," she snapped. "At least *I* didn't get on their mother about child labor laws."

"Well, it's wrong," Beau said in his own defense.

"And not at all relevant to this current situation," she pointed out.

"You know," Camden interjected around a mouthful of Thin Mints, "I hate to agree with fang face, but the two of you look good as a couple." He shoved an entire cookie into his mouth. "Fight like one, too," he mumbled, crumbs spraying out of his mouth.

"I told you," Beau said, tipping a Do-si-do in Camden's direction.

Bradley's eyes narrowed at him. "Why are you eating those anyway?" she asked as an excuse to change the subject away from their coupledom. "Aren't those cookies a symbol of child labor in your sick, twisted head?"

"If you say it's cool, I trust you." Beau gave her a devilish grin. "I can't help that I'm so out of touch with modern society. Didn't you say you were going to catch me up on the things I didn't experience in the past couple decades?"

She pointed an accusing finger at him. "I wasn't talking about cookies and you know it."

Beau's eyes darkened. Part of his expression was desire, the other something scarier. "I want you to show me everything. I want to experience the world through your eyes," he said with feeling thick in his voice. "I want to experience you."

Bradley felt her heart melt at that statement. He wanted more than just sex from her. It seemed he did want them to fall madly in love with each other . . . and that was the scary factor. Could she really let herself go and fall in love with this man, a killer . . . a vampire? The dull thumping of her heart told her that she could, that she was already partially down that road.

"What *were* you talking about?" Camden asked in interest.

"Huh?" came Bradley's confused reply.

"What did you intend to catch him up on?"

Her eyes widened. She couldn't tell Camden she'd planned to help Beau make up for sixty-five years of abstinence. Thinking quickly, she blurted out, "Wrestling!"

Camden blinked in surprise. "Wrestling?"

"Yeah," Bradley rushed on, liking the idea. "He doesn't even know who Edge is, and Edge started out in a faction with a vampire! You would think that would attract his attention, but no! Vampires," she scoffed, "always out after dark. That doesn't leave much time to watch *Raw*."

Camden's eyes slid skeptically to the vampire in question.

Beau shrugged in admission. "It's true. I do not watch wrestling."

"You don't?" Camden cried, green eyes wide with shock as he bought into the lie. "You would think a vampire would be addicted to something so violent." He shook his head in disbelief. "And you don't know who Edge is? He's the Rated R Superstar."

"Sounds like a porn star gimmick if I ever heard one," Beau commented.

"No," Camden corrected, "that was Val Venis." When Beau's eyes widened, Camden waved his hands in excitement. "Okay. Let me tell you *all* about it. First . . ."

Curling up on the bed, Bradley conceded the fact that she wouldn't be getting any alone time with Beau. Once Camden got talking about wrestling, there was no stopping him. That was perfectly fine, though. She still wasn't sure how she felt about the Beau situation. She liked him, big time, but she wasn't sure that made it okay to shamelessly throw herself at him. She needed to clear her head, think about where this was going . . . only she was so tired. It had been a crazy day. Perhaps a few hours of sleep would do her good, help her think better.

With Beau's low, sexy laugh and Camden's over enthused voice in her head, Bradley slowly drifted off to sleep.

Chapter 15

Bradley awoke lying on her back, feeling hot and flustered. As she tried to assess her surroundings, hands slid over her knees and up her thighs. With a gasp, she slid her legs up, curling them toward her chest.

A kiss was placed against the side of her knee, and Beau's voice whispered from the near darkness, "Ah, the things I long to do to this body." He was kneeling in front of her, most of his body resting between her thighs. His shirt brushed against her calves, a silent testament to how close he was to her.

Relief washed through her at the sound of his voice, and an instant later, when those words sunk in, her stomach tightened in yearning. "Beau, you scared the crap out of me," she whispered back.

"You should get used to waking up to such flattery." He kissed his way slowly up her inner thigh. "You should get used to me waking you up so you can make love to me."

Bradley shivered at the sensation of his breath hot against her leg. She closed her eyes, making a small noise of encouragement.

The past few nights, Camden had slept on the small couch in their room because he was too terrified to return to his own room. She'd been slightly relieved. It took away the possibility of throwing herself at Beau.

There was nothing stopping her now. Camden had just run out to buy some food right before she laid down for a nap. She was assuming he was still out.

Beau reached her hip and made a displeased sound in the back of his throat. "I thought I warned you about the undergarments," he breathed into the bikini string of her panties.

His teeth clamped down on the string, and Bradley sat up on her elbows with a gasp. "Surely you don't intend to..." She trailed off with a sharp intake of breath as, with teeth and fingertips, Beau began sliding her underwear down.

She fell back against the pillows, her heart racing in anticipation. "What have I gotten myself into?"

"Trouble," Beau said as he slid her underwear off of her ankles. "Loads and loads of trouble." He sat back on his heels with a wicked glint in his eyes. "I'm keeping these," he informed her, holding up the tiny pair of red panties he'd just stripped from her. He tucked them away in his pants pocket before turning his attention back to her.

Lowering himself to lie next to her, he kissed a trail along her collarbone while his hands inched under her t-shirt and up her stomach until he found her breasts. "I want to drink from you," he whispered. "I want to drink from you while your body orgasms around mine." His mouth found hers as he gently fondled her.

Bradley moaned into his mouth, arching up into his hands so that he easily cupped her breasts. "Yes," she practically begged. "Yes, do that."

"I am going-" A knock at the door broke Beau off in mid-sentence. With a groan of regret, he looked toward the offending barrier to the hallway. "-to die of sexual frustration."

Bradley looked up at him with a pleading expression. "Do we have to answer it?"

"Unfortunately," he grumbled, rolling out of the bed. He grabbed a tank top and pulled it over his head as he made his way to the door. Looking through the peephole, he let out a weary sigh. "One moment," he called gruffly. Turning to face Bradley, he ordered, "Quickly. Throw some clothes on."

She hopped into action. She ran to her bag, pulled out a jean miniskirt, and slid it over her hips. She then grabbed a bra and whipped her t-shirt off.

The sight of her breasts bare and inviting caused a groan to escape Beau's lips. "I really am going to die of sexual frustration."

Bradley glanced up at him as she slid the bra straps over her shoulders. She gave him a warm smile. "You lasted sixty-five years. You'll survive now."

He watched with longing as she slid a form fitting t-shirt over her head. "Yes, but I never had you tantalizing me before either." He eyed her wistfully, his gaze lingering on her derriere as she bent to pull on a pair of knee-high boots. Once he was sure she was properly dressed, he swung the door open.

As the door slid open, Bradley looked up in just enough time to see two men. The first she didn't recognize.

He had wavy, sandy-colored hair and hazel eyes. Perched on the end of his nose was a pair of wire-rimmed glasses. He had a pleasant smile and an air of friendliness.

The second man caused her to catch her toe on the nightstand and stumble in surprise. It was the man who had first stepped into her room the night she was attacked. He was the man she'd knocked out with her baseball bat.

"Ashton," Beau greeted cheerfully. He turned and nodded an acknowledgement to the other man. "Donovan."

"Donovan," Bradley whispered to herself. He was definitely the man who'd broken into her apartment. She remembered the name. She took a fumbling step backwards, her eyes trained on the cocoa-skinned man.

Those silver eyes met hers and she fought not to squeak in fear.

"This is the girl that has caused you to feel remorse, to have pity?" Ashton asked in interest. As he stared at Bradley, his lips tugged into a frown. "She looks like a frightened little mouse. What have you done to her?"

Beau's face took on a look of confusion. He eyed Bradley thoughtfully. "I'm not sure what has her so frazzled."

"I believe it is me," Donovan said, his voice cool and collected. "I was in on the raid of her home."

"Ah," Beau said in realization. "I see. That would explain it."

Bradley looked between the two of them, an expression of disappointment on her face. "That's it? No angered rage? No defending my honor?" She stamped a booted foot in righteous anger. "You could at least punch him in the nose or something."

Beau chuckled in amusement. "I do not think that will be necessary, little Bella." He waved a hand in the direction of the man in question. "Donovan is working undercover. He is trying to keep us informed of Craven's actions. Unfortunately, Craven only trusts Kelvin with the good stuff. Donovan gives us what he can, though."

Donovan set her with a pointed, if slightly amused, look. "During the raid, I didn't get an opportunity to sneak away and warn Beau. Instead, I entered your room first in hopes of helping you sneak out the bedroom window so Jordan wouldn't get his hands on you." He shrugged. "You knocked me unconscious before I could inform you of that plan."

Beau's eyes slid to Bradley in surprise. "You knocked Donovan out cold? Good girl." He sent Donovan an apologetic look. "Not good for you, of course, but good in that she can defend herself."

Donovan gave a nonchalant shrug of his shoulders. "I am sure my skull will heal," he teased.

Bradley felt a little guilty about knocking one of the good guys out, but she wouldn't apologize for defending herself.

Ashton drew the topic away from Donovan's head injury by looking about the room and asking, "Where is the other human?"

"Camden?" Beau asked, striding over to the small table in the room and sinking into a chair. "He ran to McDonalds." He held a hand out to Bradley who instantly moved to his side. Taking her hand, he pulled her into the seat next to him.

Ashton's eyes widened. "He went out? Don't you find that to be unnecessarily dangerous?" He sank down into a chair across from them, his expression full of concern. "Something could happen to him."

Beau slumped down in his chair and gave a laid back shrug. "He'll be fine." His gaze slid over Ashton, his expression accusing. "For a human lover, you seem to forget that they need to eat. The girls that peddle the cookies were here last night, so we were able to eat those earlier, but the humans needed something else."

Ashton's eyebrows rose comically. "The girls that peddle the cookies?"

"Girl Scouts," Bradley informed him with an affectionate smirk in Beau's direction. "They've been stopping by every day after school because Beau always pays them with a fifty."

Beau shrugged as if this didn't concern him, then slid into a wicked grin and added, "Besides, Camden is far too annoying to get himself murdered. Without him, who would be left to complicate my life?"

Bradley pursed her lips and gave him a disappointed

look.

Realization lit Beau's eyes and he patted her shoulder. "I'm sorry. I forgot you, little Bella." Turning to Ashton, he said, "How could I forget that Bradley would still be around to make my life more problematic?"

Bradley's expression turned into a glare that he conveniently ignored.

"Maybe you should call the human to make sure he's all right," Ashton commented in an attempt to change the subject to something less likely to cause a fight.

Not appreciating his friend's effort in the least, Beau made a disgusted noise in the back of his throat. "That's just what I want to do," he grumbled sarcastically, but reached into his pocket for his cell phone. Instead of a phone, his hand emerged from his pocket with a pair of red, lace panties.

All eyes in the room were drawn to the incriminating scrap of fabric.

While an awkward silence filled the room, Beau slid his gaze to Bradley. He gave her a lecherous look, his mind filled with the knowledge that she wasn't wearing anything under her skirt.

Donovan finally broke the hush. "I see why Beau likes her so much," he teased. "That would make anyone rethink their loyalties."

This drew Beau's attention away from Bradley. "Wrong pocket," he said casually, stuffing the underwear back into his pants.

Bradley sunk low in her seat, planning to die of mortification. Lucky for her, Camden chose this moment to return, drawing everyone's thoughts away from her underwear.

"I come bearing Big Macs and Quarter Pounders," Camden called cheerfully as he strolled through the motel door. "Beau does not shop from the Dollar Menu." He tossed a bunch of bags to the table before running back out for a tray of drinks.

"Eat up," Camden encouraged. "There's more than enough for everyone." He plopped down in a seat between Ashton and Donovan, not looking too concerned with the new arrivals. His attention was fixated on the Big Mac he pulled from one of the bags.

Ashton grabbed a burger for himself and tossed one to Donovan. "Beau makes me fund the majority of his trips," he griped, though his voice was light with humor. "He's got no reason to shop off the Dollar Menu when he's spending my money."

Donovan chuckled. "He's an anti-hero, isn't he? He needs a paycheck to convince him to do good deeds. He can't save humanity out of the goodness of his heart."

"Hey," Beau cried in his defense. "If I remember correctly, *you* get paid as well," he directed at Donovan.

Donovan shrugged as he bit into his burger. "I'm the one putting my neck on the line. If Craven knew I was a double agent..." He shook his head, obviously not even wanting to think about it.

"You put your neck on the line?" Beau asked. "Please remember it was me that nearly had my skull bashed in at the Holiday Inn."

"You're both greedy," Ashton said, solving the argument. "Now eat."

Trying to hide her smirk, Bradley climbed to her feet. She leaned across the table and began riffling through one of the bags. "What do you want?" she asked Beau.

His voice came back thick and sensual. "The hunger I have has nothing to do with human food."

She glanced over her shoulder to Beau, a question in her eyes. She found him staring wolfishly at her bare legs and denim-clad backside. Grabbing a Quarter Pounder from the bag, she shoved it against his chest. "Down boy," she advised, though she was fighting a pleased grin.

When everyone had their food, the room became silent for a moment while everyone filled their empty stomachs. It wasn't until Camden finally seemed to realize there were newcomers in their presence that anyone spoke. He glanced at Donovan in surprise and swallowed the food in his mouth. "Dude, your eyes are, like, wicked crazy."

Donovan shot an amused look to Beau before saying, "Yeah."

Camden took another large bite of his burger and spoke around a mouthful of beef. "So, what are you then? Are you a vampire too? Are you just some weird guy with colored contacts? What's the deal? Spill."

"I'm a werewolf," Donovan replied, voice cool and unruffled at his admission. "I was born with 'wicked eyes' that never looked quite human."

Camden bobbed his head, not seeming worried that he was in the presence of a werewolf. "Cool."

Rolling his eyes, Beau turned the subject over to the topic of their mission. "I hope to be able to find Craven within a week. We can't let him slip through our fingers this time. The two of you," Beau said to Ashton and Donovan, "can stay here and do research tomorrow evening. I have to go out."

"You're leaving," Bradley asked in concern. She'd gotten so used to having him around. The thought of not having him watching over her made her nervous.

"I have a date," Beau informed them.

Donovan's eyebrows rose in surprise. "You have a date?" he asked in disbelief. "Now? In the midst of all this chaos?" He shook his head. "You who doesn't date, ever, picks now as the time to decide to start?"

Beau nodded in confirmation. "I promised an adorable Jets fan that I'd escort her to the Sunday night game for her brother's birthday."

Bradley's eyes widened in surprise at his statement. "You remembered!" Leaning over in her seat, she gave him a quick kiss on the cheek.

The smell of her perfume, the caress of her lips against his skin, raised primal urges in him, which Beau fought hard to extinguish. "Yes, well," he said brusquely, "you refused to see reason and insisted on going to this stupid game. Seeing as I am trying to keep you alive, I have no other choice but to escort you."

"Well, I appreciate it," Bradley said sweetly. She placed a hand on his thigh as she said it, her blue eyes sparkling in gratitude.

Bradley exuded innocence and trust. She was beautiful. She was sweet and angelic...and everything Beau had been yearning for in life. He felt himself growing aroused at the soft brush of her fingers against his leg and took a large bite of his burger to distract his lower extremities.

He realized in that instant that even if he killed Jordan Craven and every last one of his men, he would never be able to let Bradley go. There was no way he could go back to his life of loneliness. He lived for her smile, her girly giggles, her delight. He needed her in his life. Now he only needed to convince her that she needed him, as well.

Chapter 16

Bradley sent another anxious glance to the entrance of their section, waiting for Beau to appear and join her at their seats. The Jets game had started ten minutes ago and there was still no sign of him.

When they had arrived at the stadium, it was still light outside. Beau had instructed that she leave him in the trunk of Camden's car and he'd join her at dusk. Though it was just beginning to get dark, she was starting to worry. What if he didn't realize it was dark yet, or couldn't get out of the trunk and he was trapped in there? There was a little crawlspace between the backseat and the trunk, but what if he couldn't fit through and he was stuck?

"What kind of man stands up a girl without any word?" Bradley's brother, Adrian, asked, his voice thick with accusation as he pulled her out of her thoughts.

"He's not standing me up," Bradley shot back, nervously glancing toward the steps that led to their section.

"Who shows up late to something like this?" Adrian continued, his voice full of annoyance. He had a sour look on his face, and his wife, Katie, elbowed him in the stomach to get rid of it.

"I told you. He had to work. He'll be here as soon as he can." Bradley bit her lip, wanting to say something more to defend Beau, but she knew her brother would never understand.

Adrian had the perfect life. He loved his job. He loved his home, his pets, and his perfect wife. He was good-looking with his short, spiked blond hair and blue eyes to match his sister's. His wife was just as attractive with her shoulder length blond hair and beautiful gray eyes. Her boobs were perky, and her hair was bouncy. There wasn't a single flaw between the two of them. They were the perfect, all American couple. You could almost make out the halos around their heads.

There was no way Adrian would understand her dilemma. She could just imagine saying, *Adrian, the guy I've been sort of seeing is a vampire. By the way, I think I'm falling in love with him even though he likes to kill people and will never age while I grow old and die. Oh, and Grandma might have been a witch.* Yeah. That wouldn't go over well.

"What work is that important? You said he's a historian. History's not going anywhere. Whatever he's doing could have waited until tomorrow," Adrian griped. His eyes narrowed in suspicion as another complaint occurred to him. "How old is this guy anyway? Shouldn't you be dating a college student your own age?"

Bradley's mouth opened, but she didn't know how to answer him. She couldn't tell him that Beau was four hundred, and she wasn't quite certain of how old he'd been when he died. "Beau is...twenty-"

"Eight," Beau's voice answered as he walked up the stairs toward their seats.

"Twenty-eight?" Adrian asked in disapproval as Bradley stood to greet her date. "Can't get women your own age?"

Bradley shot her brother a warning glare, but Beau handled the comment smoothly.

"No other woman alive holds a candle to your sister," Beau informed him. "Her beauty is ageless."

While Bradley smirked in delight at his comment, Adrian scowled.

Bradley was wearing a wool winter hat with a Jets logo in the center. It had long ear covers with tie strings that she left undone, hanging past her shoulders.

Beau tugged playfully on the ear covers and leaned down to give her a quick, but firm kiss. "Sorry I'm late."

Bradley was surprised by the kiss. She hadn't realized they were up to the casual public kiss. It actually kind of warmed her heart.

Reaching inside his jacket, Beau pulled out a card and handed it to her.

She sent him a questioning look as she eyed the envelope almost suspiciously.

Beau sent her a wide-eyed expression of innocence, refusing to comment.

She returned her puzzled look to the envelope in her hand as they took their seats. With one last bewildered glance to Beau, she opened it. Inside was a Halloween card with a cheesy vampire in a purple cape on the cover. The inside read, 'You're My Type'. Bradley's eyes lifted to his in surprise. "You went back to Wal-Mart? But you hate Wal-Mart."

"I do hate Wal-Mart, but I hated the fact that I had to show up late tonight even more." He had stopped by Wal-Mart the previous evening when he and Donovan had run out for a few supplies. He hadn't liked leaving Bradley for even that half hour, but he'd trusted Ashton to keep her safe. The delighted look in her eyes right now made that entire trip worth it.

Adrian rolled his eyes. "He didn't even sign it."

"The card pretty much says it all," Bradley came back with a mischievous smile to Beau.

Adrian rolled his eyes once again, but didn't make any further comments.

As she shifted in her seat to get comfortable, Bradley slipped her hand into Beau's. She smirked at the way his fingers twitched, and at the look of surprise on his face. "It's as if you don't expect me to be nice to you," she whispered so her brother wouldn't hear.

"Let's just say I'm pleasantly surprised."

She studied his profile for a moment, a small smile on her lips. "I'm pleasantly surprised, as well."

Beau's upper lip tugged into a slow grin, and he leaned down to give her another quick kiss.

"Get a room," Adrian grumbled.

Bradley was about to tell him to stick it where the sun didn't shine when the game's announcer yelled, "Touchdown Jets!"

Jumping to her feet, Bradley let out what could only be described as a battle cry. She hopped around for a while before reaching down to pull Beau to his feet. "Celebrate," she ordered as she began a touchdown dance.

Laughing, Beau gave a more subdued clap. It was so nice to see Bradley smile, to see something other than fear and anxiety on her pretty face.

Adrian was giving Beau a suspicious look. "You don't

seem too thrilled about that touchdown."

"Oh, he's not a Jets fan," Bradley explained, shaking her head in disappointment.

Adrian's eyes narrowed. "Not a Jets fan?" The disgust was evident in his expression. "What kind of man doesn't like the Jets?" He gave a snort. "And he's a historian to boot," he grumbled, complaining about Beau's career choice.

Beau, not actually being a historian, ignored the jab at his fake profession. "I do like football. I just prefer to cheer for a team with potential, like the Steelers."

Bradley elbowed him in the gut for his insult to her team.

"The Steelers?" Adrian asked snidely. "What's so great about the Steelers?"

"The seventies. Need I say more?" Beau challenged.

"The seventies? Dude, we weren't even alive in the seventies," Adrian pointed out.

Beau's face took on a look of stunned surprise as he realized that the others hadn't even been a thought when the Steelers were busy winning their first four Super Bowls. "Well...that...that's true. Good point."

Bradley wrapped an arm around Beau's waist. "Eh, so he likes the crappy Steelers," she told her brother. "It's an obstacle, but I've decided I like him anyway."

Beau's eyes narrowed, a flash of threat in their depths. "The crappy Steelers?" As they sat back down, he whispered in her ear, "Just wait until I get you back to the motel. You're going to wish you never said that."

"Oh, no," Bradley teased. "Don't hold me down and touch me with those magical fingers of yours."

"I'm going to touch you with a lot more than that," he promised.

"I can hardly wait," she practically purred. She shot a quick, guilty look toward her brother before giving Beau a wink. Her attention swiftly returned to the game as the Jets got an interception. She jumped to her feet once again, clapping and screaming her approval. When the crowd began chanting for their team, she merrily joined in. "J-E-T-S! Jets! Jets! Jets!" she chanted, pumping a fist in the air.

Beau reluctantly dragged himself to his feet and raised an eyebrow at her in amusement. "Ingenious," he teased.

She poked him in the ribs, her nose crinkled in delight. "I'll make a Jets fan out of you yet," she declared.

Beau wrapped an arm around her shoulders and leaned down to kiss her. "You can try," he challenged.

She leaned in against him, all thoughts of the Jets leaving her as his mouth pressed warmly to hers. "Mmm," she mumbled. When he pulled back, she looked up at him, her stomach fluttering in delight at the playful glimmer in his dark blue eyes. "I never back down from a challenge," she informed him, her heart thumping at the sight of a genuine smile on his normally serious face. Things might be hectic, but the Jets were winning and Beau was at her side. Life was good.

Chapter 17

The game was over and the Jets had won. Beau was glad for that, too. He'd never seen Bradley in such a good mood. Her frown was gone, replaced with a giddy smile.

They'd stayed after the game for fireworks.

Beau couldn't recall if he'd ever seen fireworks before. It seemed like it should be impossible for him not to have seen them, seeing as how he was a creature of the night, but he'd never stopped to enjoy something so simple.

He felt fingers brush along his cheek and glanced down to see Bradley staring up at him.

"You look so...enthralled," she said with a soft, bemused smile.

"I've never watched fireworks before," he replied, sounding almost bashful.

Her face filled with surprise, and then she leaned in against his arm. "Well, I'm glad you're here to see them," she said, putting her head on his shoulder.

The scent of her shampoo drew his attention away from the colorful bursts in the sky. He fought the urge to bury his face in her silky curls. It hit him that there were other simple pleasures he'd been denying himself over the years, like romantic companionship. Bradley made his heart ache over the loneliness he'd let himself suffer through. He suddenly didn't know how he'd survived without her adorable presence in his life.

As if sensing he was watching her, Bradley lifted her eyes to look at him again.

He gave her a tender smile before returning his gaze to the fireworks display. He'd never noticed how much he'd been missing in life. He'd filled his time with death and violence, in essence, becoming a workaholic. If this night was any indication, he missed playing human every once in a while. He missed companionship and the feel of a woman in his arms. When Bradley touched him, he felt less cynical, less...detached from everything. He pondered all of this as the fireworks lit up the night sky.

Before Beau had fully sorted out his thoughts, the show was over.

Bradley took his hand and began forcing her way through the crowd of people attempting to get back to their cars. Over her shoulder, she yelled out to her brother, "Dinner?"

Adrian nodded before yelling back, "The usual place?"

She bobbed her head in agreement.

Without another word to each other, Bradley and Adrian went their separate ways, each heading out the exit closest to where they were parked.

Bradley knew the stadium like the back of her hand and it didn't take her long to guide them back to the parking lot where they'd left Camden's car. As she wove through rows of parked cars, Bradley kept a tight grip on Beau's hand.

He followed after her, keeping a watchful eye on their surroundings as the number of people around them continued to decline when others reached their vehicles. When they finally got to a spot where they had relative privacy, Beau tugged on Bradley's hand, pulling her to a stop. He then gathered her up against his chest. "I've been wanting to do this for hours," he informed her as his mouth closed over hers.

Bradley's body molded against his, her arms sliding around his neck. "And here I thought I was the only one."

He smiled against her lips. "Most definitely not." He slid his arms around her, his hands pressed to her lower back. He let himself enjoy the kiss, taking delight at the small noises of happiness Bradley made, but he kept his guard up. He could never fully let it down, not when they were out in the open and exposed like this. It was because of his constant vigilance that he saw a shadow moving toward them out of the corner of his eye. Silently, he removed one hand from Bradley's waist and slid it inside his jacket, his fingers tightening around a stake.

Feeling him reaching inside his jacket, Bradley pulled back slightly, a question in her eyes. "What-"

Before she could finish the sentence, Beau swooped in,

kissing her with even more passion, nipping on her lower lip to keep her from talking. If she realized he was aware of someone approaching them, the other person might catch on by her change in behavior. Trying to keep her distracted, Beau's kisses became demanding and a little forceful.

She let out a soft whimper, relaxing against him as she completely forgot about what she'd been about to ask.

Beau was slightly distracted by that whimper, but he was trained for combat, trained to stay focused. He forced himself to stay aware of the man a few yards in front of them instead of getting caught up with the gorgeous brunette in his arms.

When the person was a few feet away, Beau lifted Bradley's right leg around his waist and spun her out of harm's way. He forced her up against the side of a car as if in the throes of passion. The man still had no clue Beau knew he was there, and Bradley had no clue there was any danger around them. That would make this kill easier.

He ripped his mouth away from hers, lowering his lips to her neck. Through a wall of hair, he watched their would-be assailant in the reflection of the car window.

The man was a vampire, one of Craven's.

In the man's hand, Beau could see a small knife. He grinned. The man had brought a knife to a stake fight.

Beau thought of letting the man stab him before he killed him just to prove how useless a knife would have been even if he'd gotten a jab in. He threw that idea out solely for the fact that he couldn't show up to dinner with a knife wound. So Beau waited until the man was nearly on top of him before driving the stake he'd gotten from his jacket pocket back into the vampire's chest.

The vampire gave a surprised holler of pain before exploding into dust.

Bradley gave a startled yelp and stared at the disintegrating vampire in horror. Her eyes widened as the knife the vampire had been holding fell to the ground with a clatter. "You...he..."

Beau slid his arm around her shoulder. "As much as I'd love to stand here and kiss you all night, your brother is waiting."

Bradley let Beau walk her to the car and tuck her into the passenger seat. When he'd climbed in and started the car, she said. "You killed him."

"In all fairness," Beau came back, "he tried to kill me first."

This statement seemed to calm Bradley because she became silent, only speaking to give him directions. A short while later when they reached the restaurant, she asked, "What happens when Adrian or Katie ask us a personal question? Like stuff about you?"

Beau gave a casual shrug as he pulled into a parking space. "We tell them the truth." He paused in thought. "Well, as much of the truth as we can without mentioning that I'm a vampire...or the fact that I kill people for a living."

"I'm sure you realized by my brother's grilling that I went with the story you told me when we first met. I told them you were a historian."

"Good girl." Reaching out, he placed his hand over hers. "You'll be fine. You faced down an attack from supernatural beings a couple days ago. Dinner with big brother should be a piece of cake compared to that."

With a smile, Bradley leaned over to give him a quick kiss on the cheek. "Thank you. You're absolutely right. What's dinner with my brother when there are evil men out to kill me?"

Beau's mouth tugged into a frown as he shut off the car. "Well, when you say it like that, it makes my pep talk sound bad."

Bradley laughed as she climbed out of the car. "I can't let you know how much your little speech actually relieved me. I have to keep you from getting a big head. You're impossible to deal with now."

He shook his head with a playful laugh. "Remind me again why I didn't just kill you."

She met him at the front of the car and threw her arms around his neck. Pulling him down for a slow, passionate kiss, she pressed her body along the front of his.

"Oh," Beau practically growled out, his arms going around her waist, "that's why."

Bradley pulled back with a giggle. "That and the fact that you find me too adorable to kill."

"Now who's got the big head?" he asked with a crooked grin.

She leaned forward and brushed her lips across his. "You

do," she accused, giggling against his mouth. "You're far too arrogant for your own good."

"Get a room," Adrian's voice grumbled from behind them. "Thank goodness we haven't eaten yet, or I would have just vomited."

Beau gave a quiet groan of disappointment at being interrupted before slowly removing his mouth from Bradley's. "Adrian!" he said brightly, ignoring the other man's comments. "I didn't realize you were here yet."

"Of course we're here," Adrian said tersely. "We've been waiting forever for the two of you."

Beau's expression became apologetic. "That would be my fault. I ran into an old acquaintance of mine in the parking lot. It was more like one of those acquaintance of an acquaintance type deals. Quite boring, but a necessary evil."

Bradley shot him a look. Necessary evil? He had the evil part right. The man had tried to kill them!

Adrian's eyes narrowed, but he couldn't find anything snide to say about Beau's excuse.

Both men stared at each other in a challenging silence, both standing their ground, unwilling to look away.

Katie put a dainty hand on Adrian's arm, her long, perfectly polished nails gleaming in the light shining from the restaurant. "Aid, don't you think we should go inside? My toes are getting cold."

Katie's angelic, faultless voice seemed to break the spell. Both men stepped back, the hostility washed from their faces.

"Of course, honey," Adrian said with a dimpled smile to his wife. Putting a hand on her shoulder, he guided her inside.

On her way past, Katie gave Bradley a crooked grin and rolled her eyes. "Men," she mouthed silently.

Bradley grinned in return. It was hard to dislike Katie for being perfect when she was so nice. Following after them, she nudged Beau with her elbow. "What happened to this being easy? Your hackles are up already."

Beau rolled his eyes and mumbled something unintelligible.

Standing on her tiptoes, Bradley kissed his chin. "If you be nice through dinner, maybe I'll let you eat your dessert off of me," she teased.

Beau's blue eyes darkened at that suggestion. "You don't play fair."

With a giggle, she maneuvered them over to the table where Adrian and Katie were sitting down. "I've got to keep you on your toes. Nobody likes a lazy vampire."

"Lazy my ass," Beau retorted. "You're trying to kill me with sexual frustration." They had reached the table at his last comment.

Katie snickered, but politely chose not to comment on Beau's sexual frustration.

Adrian, luckily, had been busy talking to the waiter.

After a quick perusal of the menu, they ordered, not wanting the waiter to get away and forget about them due to the crowd pouring in from the football game.

As soon as the waiter was gone, Adrian turned to Beau, trying to make his expression curious. He failed miserably. Everyone at the table could tell it was an interrogation. "So...Beau," Adrian said, feigning casualness as he tapped his menu against the tabletop. "A historian, huh? That's an odd career choice."

Beau, not at all perturbed, flashed a grin that made Bradley's knees wobble. "I was a big Indiana Jones fan. He inspired me. He made being a historian look pretty badass."

Bradley knew Adrian couldn't have a complaint about Beau's explanation because he found Indiana Jones to be pretty badass, as well.

While Adrian pouted over his lack of a justification to dislike Beau, the vampire in question asked, "So, what do you do?"

Adrian waited while the waiter plunked down their drinks. "I'm an architect," he finally replied, eyes narrowing at Beau.

Putting a hand on her husband's arm, Katie gushed, "He's designed some very gorgeous buildings. I'd never thought that buildings could be beautiful, but what Adrian does is a work of art."

"Quite the talented family," Beau commented. "One is very artistic, the other brainy. You," he said to Adrian, "make buildings while Bradley makes bombs."

Bradley nearly spit her drink out. "I was not making a bomb!" The feigned look of surprise on Beau's face made her burst into giggles. "I told you that already!" She turned to her brother to explain. "Camden spilled bleach on me in the chemistry lab, and Beau somehow got it in his head that we were being instructed by the teacher on how to build a bomb."

"Oh!" Adrian cried brightly. "You've met Camden." His brows tugged down in fake concern. "It doesn't bother you that he and Bradley are so close?"

Beau waved off the comment. "Nah. Camden's a cool kid. I know where Bradley's heart lies, and I know the chick Camden is interested in." He gave a wicked grin. "Besides, I'm not the jealous type. I have confidence in my ability to hold a woman's attention." The tone of his voice held a slight implication that perhaps Adrian couldn't do the same.

Adrian bristled, but the waiter arrived with their food to distract everyone from Beau's cocky remark.

Bradley wasn't fooled by the content manner in which everyone started in on their food. The tension in the air was thick. Under the table, she smacked Beau in the thigh.

He ignored the slap as if he hadn't felt it, but Bradley saw his lips twitch in silent laughter. He was deliberately goading Adrian. It was entertaining to him.

As if to prove how much he was enjoying himself, Beau asked, "So how long have you two been married? If I had to take a guess, I'd have to say half a century."

Adrian's expression turned sour at Beau's teasing. "You're older than I am."

"That I am," Beau agreed with an amused chuckle.

Adrian, finding this to be another good topic to grill Beau on, asked, "And what about you? You're twenty-eight. Surely someone of your age has to have had a serious relationship or two."

At Adrian's comment, Beau's face fell, and his happy expression faded away. His eyes lost their happy sparkle as he said, "I was married before."

Bradley nearly fell out of her chair. She knew she must be gawking at him in utter shock, but she couldn't help herself. Beau, her Beau, had gotten married. She couldn't believe it.

Beau sent her a look that was a mix between apologetic and sad. "We were barely married six months before she died."

Katie gave a horrified gasp, her hands moving to cover her mouth.

"Hey," Adrian said, realizing he'd gone too far with his prodding. "I'm sorry." His voice held real regret, and his eyes glanced toward his sister for forgiveness for his pushiness.

Beau's gaze slid to him. "It's all right. You didn't know." He shrugged. "Besides, it was a long time ago."

After that, the evening seemed to go much smoother. Adrian and Beau actually became civil with one another. Things went better than Bradley expected despite Beau and Adrian's nightmarish beginning attitudes. After dinner, Adrian even encouraged her to call and set up another double date.

When she finally climbed into the car, Bradley sank into the seat with a content sigh. "That went well."

Beau nodded as he started up the car. "It did. We did not get attacked at all during dinner."

Bradley made a *tsking* noise and slapped his arm. "Is that all you think about?"

"That's what I'm paid to think about."

While Beau pulled onto the road, Bradley eyed him thoughtfully. "You were married?" she asked, finally voicing what had been on her mind since it had been mentioned.

Beau spared her a quick glance before returning his gaze to the road. "Like I said, it was a long time ago, over four hundred years."

"It was when you were human," she guessed.

"Eight years before I became this," he revealed.

"Oh." Bradley shifted in her seat so she could stare up at him. "I'm sorry."

"Like I said, it was a long time ago...and she never loved me anyway." On Bradley's horrified expression, he rushed to add, "It was an arranged marriage, and she was in love with someone else. I didn't want to be married to her either. I'd had other plans for my life, but my father insisted on it." He ran a hand through his hair, aggravated at the old memory. "I didn't want to be the reason she was unhappy. The fact that I was forced into our marriage just as much as she was actually brought us together. I never thought of her as a lover, but as a very dear friend."

His expression became sad at his next statement. "Within a few months, she contracted the plague. I tried to do what I felt was best by her. I sent for the man she was in love with and let him sit by her side as the disease claimed her life."

"That was nice of you," Bradley said, voice soft, as if

afraid speaking any louder would be disrespectful to the deceased.

"Well, no good deed goes unpunished, right?" Beau asked jadedly. "He died within a week." He shook his head in disgust. "He got it from her. If I wouldn't have sought him out, he wouldn't have died. I was married to her. It should have been me."

The car was silent for a moment before Bradley whispered. "I'm glad it wasn't you."

Chapter 18

As she and Beau entered their motel room after returning from the Jets game, Bradley looked around for any of the others. She was pleased to find the room empty. They'd passed Donovan in the parking lot where he was silently keeping watch from the shelter of his car. She assumed the others had decided to crash in Camden's room. This gave her and Beau their first bit of privacy in days.

Since Ashton and Donovan's arrival, everyone slept in shifts. They alternated doing research, making food runs, and surveying the area for any sign of threats. There were people in and out of both motel rooms at all hours. This was the first time she and Beau had been alone since before the newcomers' arrival.

Without even needing to ask Donovan, she figured that everything was safe and in order because she could hear Camden's loud snoring coming from the other room. She'd spent a fair share of sleepovers shoving socks in her best friend's mouth or plugging his nose in an attempt to quiet him down. It was impossible. At that moment, she felt kind of sorry for Ashton. Not bad enough to invite him into her room, though.

When Beau turned back around from locking the door, she was waiting for him. She did what she'd wanted to do all night. She threw herself into his arms, standing on her tip-toes to press a needy kiss to his mouth. "I wanted so badly to hate you, Beau," she admitted. She kissed him again, her body molding to the front of his. "I didn't want to believe you and your silly stories." Her arms slid around his neck, fingers brushing through his thick hair. "I can't help myself, though." She buried her face into his neck, nuzzling softly. "I want to be with you no matter how illogical it may be."

Beau grabbed her hips, pinning her against him. "Then you know how I feel," he breathed, lowering his head to plant a kiss on the tip of her nose. "I want to keep you. I know I shouldn't. I know it's wrong. You're practically a child, and you've got your whole life ahead of you, but I want you. I never want to give you up," he whispered against her cheek.

"Then don't," she breathed as his mouth closed over hers. She was so lost in the kiss that she gave a little yip of surprise when he lifted her up off the ground.

He wrapped her legs around his waist, and Bradley hooked her ankles behind his back as he marched her purposefully toward the bed.

She giggled when he tipped her backwards onto the mattress. "You're a bad influence," she accused. "I never giggle. You're turning me into a girl."

"Oh, no!" He laughed against her lips. "We wouldn't want that." Beau propped himself up on his forearm and stared down at her. "The death and violence you're okay with, but the fact that I make you feel girly bothers you."

"I've had people I'm close to die before," Bradley said a little wistfully. "Unfortunately, that's an emotion I can relate to. Being girly, though...this is alien."

"I've just got you believing in vampires. Don't bring aliens into the picture," Beau chastised, his tone playful.

Her eyes widened with intrigue. "Aliens?"

Her heartbeat picked up speed against Beau's chest, sending a thrill of arousal through him. "Before you ask, I don't know if aliens exist, and no, I've never seen one." He arched an eyebrow. "Can we get back to having sex?"

"Having sex? Is that what we were about to do?" Bradley asked mischievously, running a hand along his chest.

"Yes," he practically growled. "It is." He nuzzled along her neck, gently nibbling on her earlobe. "If you try to deny me," he whispered in her ear, "I will suck your blood!" The second half of his sentence was said in a cheesy vampire voice.

Bradley giggled once again and squirmed underneath him. "Anything but that!"

Beau groaned deep in his throat at the sensation of her moving beneath him.

"I suppose I shall have to give in to your fiendish needs," she said with a soft, affectionate smile.

"You have no idea how relieved I am to hear you say that," Beau came back breathlessly.

"What? That you have fiendish needs?"

He pretended to give her a reproachful look, then completely ignored her question. Instead, he leaned forward and kissed her, his hands running through her hair. His mouth was tender and soft, a complete turnaround from the harsh persona he used to disguise the caring man he actually was inside.

Bradley gave a content sigh into his mouth as his hands moved tenderly down her sides and over her hips. It took her a moment, but she gave out a disgusted snort when the suspicion of what he was doing hit her. "You're being gentle!" she accused. "See! This is why I didn't tell you that I'd never done this with anyone else before. I knew you'd behave like this!"

"Bella," Beau whispered, his eyes alight with amusement. "I wasn't being gentle because I thought I would hurt you." He paused, giving her a soft kiss. "I was being gentle because I love you."

At his declaration, Bradley thought her heart was going to melt. "Oh, Beau," she breathed. "I love you too."

"But," Beau interrupted, "if you don't wish for me to make tender and gentle love to you, so be it." In one swift motion, he rolled over, pulling her on top of him. "You'll just have to ride me. You can control just how hard my body is thrust inside yours."

"Holy shit, Beau," Bradley whispered breathlessly. "For someone that hasn't had sex in sixty-five years, you sure are an expert at talking dirty."

"What can I say? You bring out the naughty side in me." His eyes roved hungrily over her body. "I just hope I return the favor."

Bradley tossed him an impish grin. "Oh, you definitely bring out my naughty side." Leaning over, she nipped playfully at his nose before sitting back. She made a show of removing her hat, then dropped it over his eyes.

With a laugh, Beau tossed the hat to the floor.

"You make me want to be a bad girl," she whispered, voice husky as she lifted her shirt over her head.

His eyes were riveted to her exposed flesh, and his irises flashed with eagerness at her comment. "And you said *I* was an expert at talking dirty."

She gave him a sultry look. "You inspire me." Reaching down, she grabbed the buttons of his shirt. Wiggling around a little to tease him, she said, "You are far too clothed for my liking, Mr. Channing."

"Well, then by all means, strip me down," Beau encouraged.

She stared at him thoughtfully for a moment before releasing his shirt. "If I'm going to do this, I'm going to do it right," she purred.

He made a noise of protest when she climbed off of him, but decided it was worth it when Bradley started shimmying out of her pants. His eyes were riveted to her smooth, sleek legs as she wiggled in a dance so unintentionally erotic, it had him desperate with need.

She had kicked off her shoes when she'd jumped off the bed. Now she bent to pull off her green socks.

Beau's gaze drifted to her backside, which was barely concealed in a skimpy pair of underwear. "You are pure evil," he growled out in desire.

Straightening, Bradley blinked a set of bright blue eyes at him. "That's no way to speak if you want me to strip you down and have my way with you." She looked almost surprised by his comments. As if she had no clue how completely sexy her little striptease was. The fact that she didn't realize how attractive she was made her even more alluring to him.

"I'm sorry," Beau quickly apologized, not wanting her to stop. "Continue."

Clad in only her bra and panties, Bradley climbed onto the bed at his feet, trailing her fingers lightly over his legs. "That's a better attitude," she encouraged as she knelt beside him.

Picking up his right foot, she placed it in her lap and slid his shoe off. She unceremoniously dropped it to the floor before reaching for the other.

"You didn't untie the laces," Beau complained as his second shoe thudded to the floor.

She arched an eyebrow at him, freezing with her fingertips at the top of his sock. "Would you like to do this yourself?"

He squirmed under her piercing gaze. "I'm sorry...again. I

just have a really hard time relinquishing control to someone else. Even when I was having sex in the past, I never let anyone in like I have you, Bella."

"That's sweet," Bradley informed him as she resumed removing his socks, "but I don't want to hear about you having sex with other women." She moved to his other foot, sliding that sock off, as well. "You're over four hundred years old. It would be weird if you'd never had sex. I don't expect that. I just don't want to hear about the others."

"Once again, I'm sorry," Beau apologized, feeling as if his foot was permanently in his mouth. "I'm just not used to this relationship stuff." He paused before saying, "I may have been with my share of women, but out of those, I've only loved one."

Bradley sat back and stared at him, her heart melting. "Aw, Beau," she breathed. "That is the sweetest...you meant me, right?" she asked suspiciously.

"Of course I meant you," he said with a laugh.

"Oh...then I'm quite fond of you, too." Returning her concentration to the task of undressing him, she ran her fingers along the bottom of his foot.

He jumped, his leg twitching, and he gave her a dirty look.

"Well now," Bradley said in curiosity. "A ticklish vampire. How interesting." She grazed her nails along the bottom of his other foot, tormenting him with the feathery light sensation.

Beau twitched again, his foot jerking away from her.

Though he squirmed, Bradley could see the arousal in his eyes. He was enjoying her teasing caresses. With a wicked grin, she placed her hands on his ankles and slowly ran them up his calves. She massaged the muscles through his pants, watching in fascination as his manhood grew hard and thick, the evidence very noticeable through his trousers.

Sliding up to kneel between his knees, Bradley's hands continued upward. She kneaded her fingers into his muscular thighs. "For a corpse, you are in amazing shape," she observed.

"Thanks," he replied, distracted. He was lying back against a pillow, his blue eyes watching her intently, waiting for her next move.

With a soft smile at the eagerness in his expression,

Bradley resumed her task. She slid her hands up his legs until she reached the front of his pants. Biting her lip, she ran a hand up the hard length of him through his pants until she reached his belt buckle. The higher she moved her hands, the lower she had to put her upper body. As her hands reached their destination of his belt buckle, her barely concealed breasts brushed against the front of his legs. "I'm curious to see what kind of underwear you prefer," she said as she unbuckled his belt. "Boxers? Briefs?" Things had happened so quickly last time that she hadn't gotten the chance to take in the little details. This time around, she was going to observe every inch of him.

"Vampires do not wear boxers," was his huffy response.

"Well, sorry," Bradley drawled insincerely as she pulled his belt free from his pants. "I didn't know the undead had a no boxers law. You haven't let me look at the vampire handbook yet, so how am I supposed to know such things?"

"There is no handbook," Beau griped before realizing that she was only joking. "But you weren't serious," he added, feeling sheepish.

With a nod of her head in confirmation, Bradley tossed his belt to the floor to join the pile of already discarded clothing. She then set about tugging at his shirt to un-tuck it from his pants. Her hands slid under the shirt to run along his smooth expanse of chest before returning to his pants.

She undid the button before gripping the zipper between her thumb and forefinger. With deliberate slowness, she pulled it down and made a show of peeking inside. "Boxer briefs. Sexy."

Beau had on a pair of tight red briefs. The large bulge underneath left nothing to the imagination.

"Unbelievably sexy," Bradley added as she tugged on his pant legs until his trousers came off. Once she had his pants tossed to the side, she slowly crawled up his body, making sure to rub her chest along his as she went.

She then settled her legs around his hips, straddling him while her fingers deftly unbuttoned his shirt. She tried to ignore the feeling of him hard underneath of her, though with only a thin layer of clothing separating them, it was a challenge. While she concentrated on his upper body, she couldn't help but wiggle her lower body to rub against his, letting him know she noticed his state of desire.

Beau moaned, but didn't dare move. He stayed absolutely still as she spread open his shirt.

When she had his chest bare for her viewing, Bradley leaned down and brushed her lips across the center. Upon feeling Beau's body tighten in approval beneath her, she gave him another kiss. This time, she let her tongue flick out to caress over one of his nipples.

He let out a hiss that turned into a groan of yearning.

With a giggle, Bradley nipped at his skin. "You have no idea the things I want to do to you."

"No," Beau agreed, his voice strained, "but feel free to do every last one of them."

With a throaty laugh, she began kissing a trail down his chest. She continued down his stomach, moving to his left hip where she left a playful bite that had him arching off the bed in surprise. "Had enough?" she breathed against his hip.

"Never," came his growled response.

"Okay," Bradley said, a warning in her voice as she tugged his underwear down. "You asked for it." Giving him a grin, she lowered her head and kissed the very tip of his now exposed manhood. Slowly, she flicked her tongue out to caress the sensitive underside. Getting braver, she took part of him into her mouth, sucking gently. While she did this, her hand reached behind her to the hooks of her bra. She managed to get it undone and let it slide off her shoulders as she sat back. "I'd like to explore that further one day," she said, referring to oral sex, "but right now I need to feel you inside of me." She said it mater-of-factly, not caring if he knew how much she wanted to be with him.

"I need that, as well," Beau agreed, his voice hoarse with longing. "There's nothing more I could possibly want."

She squiggled out of her underwear without standing up, tugging with her hands and wiggling around to pull herself free of the clothing.

Beau couldn't help but laugh affectionately as she squirmed around. "I do believe I love every little thing about you," he confessed.

Bradley crawled up his body, leaving kisses as she went until she was able to slide her legs around his hips. "I kind of like you, too," she informed him with a soft smile. Holding her breath almost nervously, she positioned herself above him before slowly guiding him inside of her.

Beau let out a drawn out groan. "I can't believe I gave this up because I thought it was a disgusting, animalistic act. Adding emotional involvement to this changes everything." He stroked his hands gently along her back. "The women of my past made it possible for this to be so good between us. I know what evil lies in most people's hearts. I know that you're an angel, Bella, an angel that somehow let me into her life. I misjudged sex when I labeled it as abhorrent because of my past experiences. I've never been more wrong about something in my life."

"That's because you'd never done it with me before," Bradley teased as she tentatively began feeling out a rhythm.

"That's probably true," Beau agreed in a voice strained with desire, his hands gripping tightly to her hips.

"Uh-huh," Bradley agreed breathlessly, though she could barely follow the conversation anymore. She was too lost in the sensations that tingled through her. Her body rocked slowly on top of his, sending unbelievable feelings shooting through her. She gave a soft gasp, and her head fell back as she was overcome with pleasure. She'd never been more sensitive, more attuned to every small touch. "Oh, Beau," she rasped out as she found a rhythm that felt too good to be true. It was definitely too good for either of them to last long.

His hips bucked off the bed, driving himself deeper inside of her. "Finish, Bella," he growled out. "Finish with me."

With her eyes squeezed closed and her head tossed back, Bradley made soft whimpering sounds as her orgasm approached. She felt him finish, and it threw her over the edge. Wave after wave of pleasure slammed through her. Her body trembled around his, holding him tightly inside of her.

Beau's fingers dug pleasantly into her skin, and his chest heaved up and down.

As the last little tremors of ecstasy subsided, Bradley collapsed to his chest, her breathing just as ragged as his.

Beau held her loosely in his arms, his fingers grazing gently along her back. "I love you, Bradley," he whispered in her ear, placing a gentle kiss against her hair.

"I love you too," she said softly, contently listening to the sound of his heart thumping under her ear.

After a few minutes, Beau slid her to lie next to him in

the bed. He pulled her to him, tucking her protectively against his side. Their naked bodies were pressed intimately together, legs intertwined.

At the comfortable silence that followed, Bradley voiced the thought she'd been mulling over for a while now. "Do you really think I'm a witch? Was my grandmother actually what you claim she was?" The questions might have been out of the blue, but she couldn't stand having them nagging her thoughts any longer. If she was ever going to get any answers out of Beau, it was going to be when they were alone. Opportunities like this didn't seem to happen very often. She needed to take advantage of their seclusion from the group.

Quiet filled the room as Beau pondered over his answer. "I'm not sure what you are, Bella," he said honestly, "but there's a very good possibility that you inherited the ability to do witchcraft from your grandmother."

"How do I find out?" Her voice was soft and frightened. Believing Beau meant she would be turning her entire world upside down. Once she admitted that he'd been honest about everything he'd ever said, there was no going back to blissful ignorance. She wasn't sure she could handle much more than what she was already willing to accept as truth. Falling in love with a vampire was scary enough.

To keep the conversation light and unthreatening, Beau gave a casual shrug as if it wasn't really important. "Try doing a spell." If his little Bella was a witch, which he suspected she was, they'd either deal with it, or she'd simply refuse to look into her talents. Either way, it was her choice. There wasn't going to be any pressure involved from his end.

Bradley sat up, struggled to get her limbs untangled from his, and pursed her lips in annoyance. "I don't know any spells, Beau. If I *did*, then I'd already know if I was a witch or not."

He sat up, as well, putting a hand on her shoulder. "Calm down," he said with a chuckle. "You don't need to know the words to a spell, not unless it's a very complex one. For spells that are relatively simple, any word will do. You just have to believe in your ability."

"You sure know a lot on the subject for a creature unable to use magic," she grumbled.

Beau gave her an amused grin, silently pleased that she'd actually taken in the information he'd given her on their first dinner together. "I've worked with wizards in the past. I like to know someone's abilities and limits before I agree to work with them and let them have my back in combat."

Bradley let out a soft sigh, accepting that answer. "All right...so you're telling me all I've got to do is say it in my own words?"

"That's it," Beau said as if it was that simple.

"If it's that easy, how come I've never accidentally floated the television remote across the room or something like that?" she challenged.

"Because you have to believe in your ability. *Wishing* you didn't have to get up and cross the room does not mean you *believe* you won't have to."

Bradley gave him a look of mock annoyance. "All right, Mr. Know-It-All. Can you stop trying to impress me with all your knowledge and shut up so I can concentrate?"

He rolled his eyes. "By all means." After a beat, he added, "I recommend you start with an elemental. Try to create water or wind, something like that. Those are usually the easiest to start with."

Taking his advice, Bradley searched her mind for a word, thinking on what she wanted to do. Finally finding something she felt comfortable with, she took a deep breath and said, "Fira."

"You must believe it, Bradley," Beau instructed when nothing happened. "Envision it and concentrate."

Letting her breath out slowly, she envisioned her task. She pictured a burning ball of fire. She envisioned the flames dancing about and crackling. Once she had a good mental image of what she wanted, she repeated, "Fira."

A few sparks erupted in midair. They fell like hot embers to the bed and sunk into the comforter, smoke billowing out in a thin stream a moment later.

"I did it!" Bradley cried in delight. "I did a spell!"

Beau gave a yelp of alarm and began batting at the blankets. "You're sharing a bed with a vampire and you created fire? You thought fire was a good idea?" Small flames had broken out, but Beau managed to beat them back before they did too much damage.

Bradley was busy frowning at the air. She lifted a finger and touched the spot where the sparks had sprung forth. "I expected more, though. I was trying to make a decent sized fireball, and all I got was sparks. I'm not very good."

"Oh," Beau said sarcastically, "so you were trying to murder me, not just scare me shitless."

"Don't be so dramatic."

Beau harrumphed, but said, "It was your first spell. You can't expect fireballs on your first attempt. Give it a few months and you'll be a full-blown arsonist." His eyes squinted thoughtfully. "Fira?" he asked.

She looked sheepish. "I played a lot of Final Fantasy as a kid." Before Beau could ask about her video game obsession, she gave a little pout and leaned forward to brush her lips against his. "Enough talk about magic," she admonished. "You should be giving me all the sexual pleasures you can think of while we've actually got some time alone. We've both been deprived for a very long time."

Thoroughly distracted, Beau's lips curved into a wicked grin. "I like that plan," he said as he pulled her toward him. Without warning, he flipped her onto her back and crawled up her body, crouching above her as if perched for attack. "I like it a lot."

As Bradley wrapped her arms around his neck, she said, "Storm!" An instant later, tiny droplets of water began sprinkling down onto them. It wasn't a full out storm, but she was new to this witch stuff. Like Beau said, she needed to work at it to get bigger results. "I love this witch thing!" she gushed in excitement.

Beau laughed and shook his head, tiny drops of water spraying from his hair. "We've got to teach you some less extreme words before you get the hang of this, or you'll either drown yourself or burn down the building you're in."

Bradley giggled and gave him a playful, smacking kiss. "I trust that you'd save me."

Chapter 19

Bradley and Beau stood in front of the connecting door to Camden's motel room. They'd finally managed to crawl out of bed and throw on enough clothing to look presentable. Beau knew his appearance screamed out the fact that he'd just had sex. His hair was slightly messy, and his attitude was too positive. He smelled as if he had rolled in the flowery scent that always followed Bradley. Smugly, he realized that he pretty much had, and he didn't care who knew it. Right now, he had more important things to worry about than Bradley's perfume lingering on his skin. He needed to discuss the previous night's events with Ashton and Donovan.

After being spotted last night, he knew they had to make a move soon. Waiting around any longer was going to get someone killed. He shouldn't have even waited this long, but he'd gotten greedy.

He reached for the door handle when Bradley threw her arms around his neck, stopping him. "I don't want to go see the others. I want to spend some more time with you."

Smiling, Beau leaned down to give her a quick kiss. "I would love to stay here all day with you." He gave her another kiss, this one lasting longer than the first. "Unfortunately, it is not a good thing that we were followed to that football game last night. By the time we got back, it was too close to dawn to safely switch hotels. I will need to discuss last night with Ashton and Donovan, see what they think we should do about our situation."

Bradley pouted, but gave in. "All right, but when all these death threats are over, you owe me some quality alone time."

"Sweetheart, with me, the death threats never end."

"Awesome!" Bradley cried, feigning delight. She swatted

a hand against his chest. "You know that's not a good thing, right?"

He gave a noncommittal shrug. "Life with me is never boring," he offered, looking for a positive in the circumstances.

As if to prove this point, the door in front of them was suddenly yanked open, and Camden came barreling in with a panicked look on his face. "There is a group of angry dudes outside my room right now that are about to kick the door in." There was a loud cracking sound, and Camden corrected himself. "Change that. They're *in* my room, and they've already kicked the door in."

Beau gave a grumble of annoyance and stalked into Camden's room. "Same as the last time, Bella. Aim for the heart," he tossed over his shoulder. As he entered the room, Beau's eyes swept over the intruders. There were four vampires he didn't know. Behind them was Donovan, and then Kelvin, bringing up the rear of the group.

As they entered the room, Ashton jumped out from behind the door and drove a broken chair leg through the back of one of the vampires.

The leg burst through the front of the vampire's chest, and a moment later, he disintegrated into dust. He was dead before he even realized he'd been in any danger.

Ashton skirted away, putting a little distance between himself and the remaining assassins.

Beau almost burst into a pleased laugh. He highly doubted Kelvin had expected Ashton to be with them. He also knew that Kelvin anticipated Donovan having his back. Essentially, Kelvin had just walked himself into a trap.

Bradley's hand gently grabbed Beau's forearm. "Why are you smiling?" she asked, almost in horror.

"Because this is going to be fun," he answered as if that should already be obvious.

"If you say so," Bradley said reluctantly, perturbed by the eager look on Beau's face. He looked far too happy for someone that was under attack.

Camden shot Bradley an amused look. "Your boyfriend's a little scary. You know that, right?"

She shrugged, feeling perplexed. She was torn between feeling relieved that Beau was a good enough fighter to keep them safe and being concerned that he found killing so enjoyable.

Catching her expression, Beau laid a hand on her shoulder, his eyes serious. "If this is too much for you now, you should go lock yourself in the bathroom and stay where it is safe until this is over, because this is only going to get much uglier." His eyes flicked to Kelvin, who was staring at the destroyed vampire's ashes in surprise. "Especially for him." There was worry in his eyes that clearly said he was afraid his entire life might be too frightening for her. He gently brushed the back of his hand along her cheek. "Are you with me, Bella?"

Bradley gulped, but nodded. She didn't like the way Beau had said things were going to get bad. It was as if he knew something, something terrible, but wasn't going to say it aloud.

"Good," Beau said. "Don't forget. Aim for the heart." With that, he strode forward toward one of the remaining vampires. Flipping a stake out of his suit jacket pocket, he attempted to drive it through the vampire's chest.

The vampire barely managed to move out of the way. Instead of going through his heart, the stake dug roughly into the flesh of his arm. With an angry snarl, the vampire lashed out at Beau, his fist barely missing his jaw.

Out of the corner of his eye, Beau saw another vampire rush at Bradley and Camden, but there wasn't much he could do while engaged in hand to hand combat with the vampire in front of him.

Camden looked terrified, but he didn't take off running back into the other room, the one that was relatively safe. He stood his ground, the skin around the corner of his eyes tightening with his nervousness.

Beau was proud of Camden's courage, but he didn't have time to comment on it because the vampire he'd been fighting swung a chair at his head. Beau ducked out of the way as best as he could, and the chair glanced off his shoulder.

Moving with lightning quick speed, Beau grabbed the vampire's arm and slammed the man against the wall. With his free hand, Beau drove his stake deep into the vampire's chest. Without waiting to watch the man turn to dust, he attempted to turn back to make sure that Bradley and Camden were okay. Before he found them, he caught a glimpse of Kelvin and Donovan, obviously the two with the highest rank amongst Jordan's attending crew, hanging back by the open doorway.

A woman carrying groceries came to an abrupt stop at the sight of a physical altercation going on inside the room. She gasped, taking a frightened step backward.

Donovan spun on the woman, a vicious growl escaping him. "Get the hell out of here!" he snarled. "You even think about calling the cops and I will hunt you down and kill you. Understand?"

The woman's eyes widened in horror, and she dropped the bag of groceries to the pavement. Spinning on her heels, she raced back to her car.

Beau had been watching the woman in concern, but quickly forgot about her as she sprinted away. Instead, he went back to looking for his friends.

The woman was peeling out of the parking lot before Beau's eyes even found the others in his group to make sure they were okay.

Beau quickly spotted Ashton battling a vampire.
Ashton didn't look as if he was going to need any help. He was doing fine on his own, though Beau could count on one hand how many times he'd been forced to fight.

Beau's eyes came to a stop on Bradley and Camden as he continued his search.

As the vampire strode toward them, Camden pulled a stake from the back pocket of his baggy pants, holding it in front of him as if trying to deter the vampire from closing the small gap between them.

The vampire was cocky, not afraid of Camden because the kid was human. He didn't even protect his chest as he approached.

His breathing shaky with adrenaline, Camden jammed the stake forward into the vampire's chest when it grabbed for him.

The vampire jolted when the stake pierced his flesh, but the wood didn't get far enough into his body to reach the heart. The vampire looked down at the stake hanging out of his chest and let out a deep, mocking laugh. "Apparently someone doesn't have enough strength to get the job done."

Camden's expression was one of unconcern. "Yeah, I was warned that might happen." Grabbing a hammer from the tool loop of his jeans, he tossed it up into the air.

The vampire's eyes followed the hammer as if in slow motion.

Before the vampire could even register what was happening, Camden caught the hammer and swung it around. It hit the stake and drove it viciously into the vampire's chest.

The vampire stumbled backwards, clutching at the murderous wood as he burst into dust.

Beau's eyebrows rose in admiration. Apparently Ashton and Donovan had been teaching the kid a few tricks.

The vampire Ashton had been fighting suddenly went sailing through the air. He hit the wall behind Camden and Bradley with a sickening thud and then slid to the ground.

Survival instincts had the vampire scrambling to his feet despite the pain. With a quickness that only the supernatural possessed, he grabbed Bradley, yanking her toward him by her throat. "I will kill her, Channing. If you or any of your friends come one step closer, I will snap her neck!" He kicked his foot into a startled Camden, driving the kid across the room and into a wall.

Beau froze, watching as Camden hit the floor with a groan. His eyes shot quickly back to Bradley. He stood rooted to the floor, unwilling to put her life in jeopardy by moving.

Bradley's eyes were wide with horror. She struggled, her eyes pleading with Beau to save her.

"I can hear her heart racing," the vampire said, licking his lips. "Thump thump. Thump thump. It makes me want to have a taste."

When the vampire's head dipped over Bradley's neck, Beau roared, "Don't you touch her!"

Behind Beau's shoulder, Kelvin laughed, taking a step forward now that he felt he had the upper hand. "Well, well. The untouchable man has a weakness."

Following Kelvin, Donovan took a few steps into the room. He continued past Kelvin, making his way over to Bradley and the vampire. "Well, well, well," he drawled lazily. "This girl must have the sweetest blood in the world if Mr. Channing is protecting her, and it, so fiercely. It makes me want to have a taste, as well."

"Don't even think about it," Beau growled.

"You are in no position to make demands," Donovan pointed out. He walked behind the vampire holding Bradley, circling him until he came to stand in front of the terrified girl. "I have the urge to tear her throat out and watch all that pretty blood flow freely until she's dead."

With one quick movement, Donovan yanked Bradley away from the vampire and shoved her in Beau's direction. He then slammed a stake through the vampire's chest.

The vampire gave a gasp of surprise that was cut off when he disintegrated.

"You should choose your allies more wisely," Donovan growled to Kelvin, his voice full of menace.

Kelvin was staring at Donovan with a look of horror when the realization that he'd been betrayed hit him. He glanced over his shoulder to see if he could make it to the door, but Ashton had snuck behind him.

Ashton swung the door shut, and it closed with a bang of finality.

Kelvin's eyes slid to Beau and his feet shifted in unease.

"You tried to have me killed," Beau said, voice dark with rage he barely held in check. "You left me tied to a tree while the sun was rising." He stalked toward Kelvin, his body radiating aggression. "You've been nothing but a hassle for me since our paths crossed. All that I could have gotten over, but you crossed my line when you put your hands on Bradley." He towered over Kelvin menacingly. "When you raided her apartment, you held her down and tried to suffocate her."

Bradley felt her blood turn to ice at the memory. Her hand went to her throat, remembering the feeling of Kelvin's hands as they squeezed down on her windpipe. She didn't know if she'd ever been more terrified in her life.

Camden was just staggering to his feet. Seeing the expression of fear on Bradley's face, he put a comforting arm around her shoulder, pulling her against him.

"You terrorized her. You stole her artifact, and now you've come to finish her off." Beau put a hand on Kelvin's shoulder, clamping down with enough force to cause pain. "You showed the woman I love no mercy. You'll get none from me."

A shudder passed through Kelvin, and his frantic eyes darted about, searching for an escape route. Beau's grip on his shoulder tightened, forcing Kelvin's gaze to return to the angry vampire.

"You're going to tell me where Craven is going and what

he plans to use the artifact for. If you don't, I will torture and disfigure you until even your own mother won't recognize your face." Beau threatened.

A steely look of determination entered Kelvin's eyes, and he clenched his jaw, remaining silent.

Beau caught the look and gave a weary sigh. "You've seen the results of what I can do. I've tortured your men for information before," he warned, voice low. "Don't make this worse on yourself than it has to be."

Kelvin's lip curled into a cruel grin. "Would you really torture me in front of your new girlfriend? Do you want her to see what kind of monster you truly are?"

Beau fought to keep his eyes from straying to Bradley. "She's been warned of my true nature. If she finds it disturbing, she can leave the room. Whether she approves or not, I will be killing you tonight."

Bradley had known going into this situation what Beau's intentions for Kelvin were, but that didn't make this any easier. Shifting nervously on her feet, she gripped the front of Camden's shirt for moral support.

Camden gave her shoulder a comforting squeeze as his green eyes slid to Kelvin, their gaze hard and unforgiving. "After what you did to Bradley, I have no problem letting Beau tear you limb from limb." Though his words were tough, Camden's voice trembled.

"That's just what I'm going to do, too," Beau promised. "I will have you begging me to kill you. In the end, you'll tell me everything I want to know. You and I both know it, so save yourself the agony."

On Beau's nod, Ashton brought over a chair, and Donovan pulled a long length of rope from his back pocket. While Beau supervised, the two men tied Kelvin to the chair.

"My, how the tables have turned," Beau said, voice chipper. "Now *I* have *you* tied up." He tapped his chin. "I'm trying to recall how I was treated while I was chained to that tree." He feigned a look of enlightenment and snapped his fingers. "Oh, yeah!" Without warning, he delivered a brutal punch to Kelvin's jaw.

The sound of breaking bone filled the air, and Bradley gave a startled gasp that was mostly drowned out by Kelvin's holler of pain.

Beau made a sound of disappointment. "I forgot that

you're human!" he lied sarcastically. "You guys break so easily! Had I thought of that, I would have started with something a little less violent." Lunging forward, he gripped Kelvin's chin in his hand. "Just tell me what I want to know!"

Kelvin made a sound of pain, and Bradley cringed, her stomach flipping.

Beau suddenly spun in her direction, his hand not leaving Kelvin's busted jaw. His gaze roamed over her face until their eyes met. While he stared into Bradley's blue depths, he said, "Ashton, take them out of here. They aren't prepared to handle this. I should only be getting fear from Kelvin. I'm getting it from three of you, as well."

Bradley dragged her eyes from his, staring down at the carpet almost in shame. She knew this needed to be done, but damn it, she couldn't watch. She couldn't stand here and act like it didn't bother her, couldn't act like the sight of Beau in his element didn't terrify her.

A hand pressed gently to her back, and with a little gasp, Bradley looked up to find herself staring into Ashton's warm, brown eyes.

"Let's go into the other room," Ashton suggested softly.

Bradley nodded her agreement, her eyes sliding to Beau's once more before she quickly looked away. As they returned to the other room, Bradley heard Beau's voice instruct, "Gag him. I don't want to chance his screaming drawing any attention."

Bradley shivered at the malicious, pitiless tone in Beau's voice. She was guided farther into the other room and was relieved for the distance that was now between her and what Beau was doing. That thought filled her with guilt. She was trying to put space between herself and Beau.

Beau was only doing the things he was to keep her safe. He was protecting her the way he best knew how.

With a weary sigh, she strolled over to the bed and sunk down onto it.

"You don't have to feel guilty about being adverse to violence," Ashton soothed. "Beau would not blame you for being uncomfortable."

Bradley looked up at him in uncertainty. "I feel like I should be back there supporting him."

Ashton grimaced. "Trust me. You don't want to watch. Besides, Beau works better when he's not worrying about someone watching over his shoulder."

She nodded, tension easing out of her shoulders. With a soft exhale, she studied Ashton's face. "You don't look like you are fond of the violence either."

"Beau had said three of us were afraid," Camden said as he sunk down into a chair, his face drawn with stress. "I take it you're the third person. Donovan looked like it was just another day at the office, so I doubt he was too frightened."

Ashton shivered as he leaned against the small table in the corner of the room. "I don't like the violence any more than either of you. I do computer work. I track down potentially dangerous artifacts. I normally avoid this step in the process."

Bradley couldn't help the grin that spread across her face. "A vampire who's a computer expert." She found it ridiculous that Beau had a cell phone. The fact that Ashton was a computer wiz was unfathomable.

Ashton flashed her a crooked grin. "I don't really fit the stereotype, do I?"

"No, you don't," Bradley admitted, her grin widening in response to his.

"Hey, wait a second," Camden cut in. "So you're the guy who tracks down people for Beau and sends him off to do the dirty work. You sent him to kill Bradley."

Ashton shot Camden a slightly annoyed look. "I try very hard to obtain items in a nonviolent manner. I try to come by the items honestly through legitimate purchases."

"Ashton was very persistent with me," Bradley admitted.

"It's only after I am certain that an individual is unwilling to cooperate that I send in Beau, and even then, I do not require the person's death. It is Beau's personal choice to kill. He has seen too many people in his line of work end up dead because of an act of mercy. I do not blame him for watching out for his own health. What he does is dangerous, and most people I send him after are known dark arts practitioners."

A muffled holler was heard from the other room, and Bradley cringed.

"They're bad people, Bradley," Ashton said quickly. "That man in there has killed more people than you can ever imagine. The items we seek are unbelievably dangerous. Beau does what he must to stay alive."

Another muffled wail of pain filtered through the door.

Bradley shifted in unease, trying to block out the sound of the man being tortured in the next room.

Ashton's eyes filled with concern. "I do not like violence, but I have come to learn that it is a necessary evil. Do not let this affect the way you perceive Beau. He cares a great deal about you. I've known him a very long time, and I can tell you that no other woman has ever affected him the way you do."

She nodded her head, feeling too emotional to speak. She loved Beau, she honestly did, but she couldn't sit here and listen to him torture another human being.

As if to remind her of what her boyfriend was doing, a pitiful moan drifted through the door.

"There has to be another way to get this information," Bradley said in desperation.

"There isn't," Ashton said with regret. "Beau's been back and forth with this group for a couple of years. He's never been able to get his hands on Craven. The man is very elusive. Having Craven's second in command is an amazing opportunity. We can't pass this up. There is no other way."

Bradley's gaze shifted to Camden, and he gave a helpless shrug.

Giving in, Bradley leaned back against the headboard of the bed. "I don't like this," she unnecessarily informed the room.

"Neither do I," Ashton came back.

With a frustrated huff, she crossed her arms under her chest. She wasn't happy with the circumstances, but she couldn't think of a better alternative. Though she was displeased with their situation, she sat back and did nothing while Beau tortured a man only a few feet from where she sat because she couldn't come up with a different plan. With each passing minute, she became more uncomfortable with the sounds coming from the next room.

The muffled screams of agony were turning into pitiful sobs.

Bradley covered her ears with her hands, but blocking out the sound didn't block out the knowledge of what was going on. Unable to take it anymore, she sprang to her feet. "We'll find another way. I'm not letting this happen." Before Ashton could stop her, she marched through the connecting doorway. "Beau—"

Just as she entered the room, Beau grabbed Kelvin's head from behind and yanked viciously, snapping bones that were vital to a human body.

Kelvin's body slumped in death.

With a startled shriek, Bradley stumbled backwards into the wall, her hands trembling violently.

"Take care of the body," Beau ordered Donovan as he strode with purpose in Bradley's direction.

Donovan gave a brisk nod. "I'll meet up with you when I'm finished."

Without a look back, Beau made his way into the other room. He grabbed Bradley by the elbow on his way past, pulling her to follow him. "You shouldn't have gone in there," he said darkly.

Before she could respond, Beau came to an abrupt halt in front of Ashton. "We know what he plans to do." His mouth tugged into a handsome frown. "He's planning on raising Dulapet Anexton."

Ashton gave a surprised gasp, but Bradley and Camden just blinked at Beau because the name didn't ring any bells to them.

"Dulapet—" Ashton began, but Camden cut him off.

"Like fighting your dog," Camden offered with a laugh. On the odd looks he received, he explained. "Duel-a-pet. Like dueling. With swords..." He trailed off. "Okay, I thought it was funny."

Giving Camden a disapproving look, Ashton continued where he'd been interrupted. "Dulapet was a vampire who used to torture and enslave humans," Ashton explained. "He claimed his goal was to eventually have supernatural beings running the entire world. He wanted to keep mortals locked up like cattle. He was responsible for the death of millions."

Bradley stared at him in stunned silence. This was bad. This was very bad. She suddenly realized why Beau had been so desperate to get the necklace locked up.

"You guys can stop him though, right?" Camden asked hopefully. "He died before. He can die again."

"Beau was the one who killed him the first time," Ashton said quietly.

"Yeah, and I got damn lucky," Beau stated. "I should have died. He had me beat, but he got cocky and made a careless move. He won't make the same mistake twice."

"Why raise someone like that?" Bradley asked in horror. "He sounds completely evil. What does this Craven guy think he's going to accomplish? Doesn't he realize that *he's* human and thus likely to be killed by Dulapet as soon as he raises him?"

"Craven is banking on Dulapet being grateful for his resurrection. He thinks he can ride Dulapet's coattails into power." Beau grimaced before adding, "They've also got a common enemy."

To steer the conversation away from how many people wanted Beau dead, Ashton asked, "Do you know where Craven's going to raise him?"

Worry lines creased Beau's forehead. "Yeah. It just keeps getting worse. There's a big, formal dance at the college tonight. He plans on raising Dulapet outside the building, then sending him in to massacre everyone in an attempt to draw Bradley, and thus myself, out."

Bradley felt as if she was going to faint. "He's going to kill everyone at the dance?" She couldn't imagine all of the people she knew at the school being murdered.

Beau nodded solemnly. "Yeah. That means we have to go now. Craven left for the dance the same time Kelvin left to get here. Who knows how many people are dead already."

It suddenly dawned on Bradley how important it had been for Beau to get that information from Kelvin. Without it, all the people at the dance would have died without even a chance of survival. One guilty man for hundreds of innocent lives. Beau had done what was necessary. It wasn't a great thing, but it was better than the alternative.

As Ashton and Camden climbed to their feet and solemnly checked their supply of stakes, Bradley took the opportunity to get a private word with Beau.

She gently grabbed the front of his shirt in her fist, clenching the fabric that rested across his stomach. Beau's eyes lowered to hers, and her heart constricted in her chest. Standing on tiptoes, she gave him a soft, lingering kiss. "Thank you for doing what had to be done, what I couldn't do."

Beau's blue eyes held so many emotions, the main one being relief. Putting his hands on either side of her face, he gave her another kiss. "You have no idea how much I love you right now."

Bradley closed her eyes, finding strength in his touch. "Let's go save some lives," she said firmly.

Chapter 20

Beau stared up at the tall building that Kelvin had described to him. Music blared from inside and happy chatter could be heard over the sound. "This is the place."

"Are you sure he wasn't lying?" Camden asked, brushing his shaggy hair out of his eyes as he looked in skepticism at the welcoming scene the dance made.

A split second later a scream tore through the air, and the music screeched to an abrupt halt.

"I think he told the truth," Beau said dryly as he started toward the doors, "and I think we got here just in time for the party."

Camden looked down at his baggy pants and t-shirt sporting, *Your girlfriend is ugly.* He grinned in amusement. "And here I am completely underdressed."

Beau's lip quirked, but he started his instructions in a completely deadpan voice. "I want you and Bradley to try to get as many people out as you can. Try to steer clear of the battle." He turned to Camden, his eyes intense. "And, kid," he said, his voice taking on a serious edge, "if something happens to me, I want you to get Bradley out of here immediately. Grab her and run. Leave town."

Camden's eyes widened in fear, but he gave Beau a nod of compliance. "I will."

Bradley wanted to protest, but they reached the doors of the building just in time to hear another panicked scream. The shout of terror made her words die in her throat.

Beau leaned in and peered through the small window in the door. "He's got vampires standing guard just inside the doors. They've got everyone trapped within the building." He let out a weary sigh. "And Dulapet is in the center of the room looking like he's at a buffet."

Bradley saw stress lines beginning to form in the corner of Beau's eyes. Whatever was going on in there was bad. She was afraid to even see, but she knew they had to go in. She couldn't afford to be afraid right now. "Let's stop him," she whispered, trying to sound brave.

Beau slid her a sideways grin at her effort. "Whoever kills the most bad guys gets the sexual treat of their choosing," he offered as a distraction for her nerves.

She couldn't help but give him a smile in return. "Deal."

"You know I'm going to win, right?" Beau asked. "Then you're going to find yourself tied to the bed covered in chocolate pudding."

"Don't count on it," Bradley tossed back. "I'm going to win and..." She grinned wickedly. "Well, I'll just leave that a surprise. I'll let you in on what I'm going to do to you after your defeat."

"You do know I love a challenge," Beau said. With that, he threw open the doors to the building. "Look who decided to crash the party, boys," he called out, his voice echoing through the cavernous ballroom.

The two vampires guarding the doors spun to face him with surprised looks on their faces. They'd obviously been expecting people to try to get out, not in.

Beau grabbed one of them by the arm and flipped him to the ground. Before the vampire could protect his chest, Beau drove a stake through his heart.

While this happened, the second vampire rushed at Bradley. He dove at her, tackling her to the ground.

Bradley had a stake in her hands. When the vampire came down on top of her, she held it up, letting him impale himself. He exploded into dust, his remains raining down on her.

Beau's face came into view as he leaned over her. "On your ass already?" he asked as he pulled her to her feet.

"One to one," she shot back in challenge. "Let the score speak for itself."

Beau's eyes filled with a smoldering look. "You are so terribly bloodthirsty."

"You think it's sexy," she pointed out.

"Unbelievably." Beau hauled her up against his chest, his lips inches from hers.

"Hello!" Ashton hollered in their direction. He was struggling to fight two vampires at the same time. They were young and inexperienced, but they had the numbers advantage. "There will be plenty of time for that later!" he complained. "Right now, I could use some help."

Camden was busy behind him, trying to evacuate some of the students while Ashton had the guards distracted.

Beau gave a sigh, his breath hot on Bradley's lips. "I suppose we will have to postpone this." He slid away from her, grabbing a stake from his jacket pocket. "Help Camden get people out," he instructed, stalking in Ashton's direction.

The vampires Ashton was fighting were young and untrained. They didn't even notice Beau as he approached. They were too involved with Ashton to pay attention to the rest of their surroundings.

Beau gave a sigh at Craven's second-rate thugs. They were babies just freshly turned. He felt almost bad as he drove a stake through one of their backs. He felt bad? Damn, he was getting soft.

As soon as the first vampire was dead, Ashton made short work of the second.

Bradley watched Ashton and Beau for a moment, completely enthralled by their swiftness and grace. Vampires could be quite beautiful even when they brought death. Shaking her head to clear it of such distractions, she turned to help Camden.

A bloodcurdling scream ripped through the air, stopping Bradley in her tracks. While the rest of her body was frozen in fear, her eyes slid to the center of the dance floor.

Jordan Craven was yanking Tyler Silver, a girl in Bradley and Camden's biology class, across the dance floor.

"Craven," Beau said between clenched teeth.

Tyler struggled against Jordan, small whimpers escaping her. "Please! Don't do this! Stop!"

Jordan shoved her toward the man that stood imposingly in the dead center of the dance floor.

The man Craven shoved Tyler to had an expression on his face that said he considered himself to be lording over everyone in the building. He held everyone's lives in his hands, and they all knew it.

"Dulapet," Beau whispered, his voice holding an edge of fear.

Bradley didn't like to hear that fear. Beau was her protector, her warrior. Something had to be downright evil to scare him.

Dulapet wasn't as tall as Beau, but he was bigger, bulkier. His skin had a bronzed look to it that made Bradley think Egyptian, but she could tell he'd lived there long before it became the civilization it was today. Though his body appeared young, he had an ancient feel about him. The scariest thing about him was the look in his eyes. They were cold, void of pity and humanity. The look in his eyes was soulless.

Tyler was shoved in front of him. She stumbled and fell to her knees, and her face rose to stare up at Dulapet. Tears welling in her eyes, she held her hands up, pleading. "Please don't hurt me," she begged. "Please. Please." Tears streamed down her cheeks, making tracks through drying blood that didn't appear to be her own.

Without an ounce of mercy, Dulapet lifted a sword into the air. His face split into a malicious grin, and he slashed it at Tyler. The blade cut through her throat, slicing through skin and muscle.

Bradley gaped in horror. She'd never seen anything so vulgar, so cruel, in her life.

Dulapet lifted the sword and licked along the blood-covered steel. "I haven't had this much fun in ages," he breathed as Tyler's body fell lifelessly to his feet. "Bring me another." His eyes scanned the group of people trapped by a circle of Craven's vampires.

The vampires were holding people in, their bodies trapping the humans like they were in a corral. Every time Dulapet requested another victim, they would break the circle just enough for Craven to reach in and grab someone out.

"That one," Dulapet said, pointing at a terrified Kristie Taylor.

Jordan Craven marched over and grabbed Kristie by the throat. "You're next, sweetheart," he said with a malevolent sneer.

Not wanting Dulapet to claim another life, everyone jumped into action.

Beau started toward Dulapet, but was quickly swarmed by a group of vampires looking to protect the ancient.

Camden had also rushed forward. He managed to get past the vampires because they were preoccupied with Beau. He shoved through the battle, making a b-line for Craven.

Camden reached Craven and tackled him, using his momentum to drive him into the floor. The two of them, and Kristie, fell to the ground in a heap of tangled legs and arms.

Bradley stood frozen in shock as Camden lifted himself to his knees and drove a fist down into Craven's face. She didn't see anything further because a vampire grabbed her from behind and swung her face first into a wall. She hit hard, but didn't have the luxury of babying her now aching wrist. She whipped back around to face her attacker only to see him turn to dust.

As the body fell away, Donovan came into view, a large stake in his fist.

Placing a hand to her pounding heart, Bradley thanked him, glad that Donovan had caught up to their group so quickly after dumping Kelvin's body.

"Yeah, well," Donovan said distractedly to her thanks as he sought out his next victim. "Beau would kill me if I let anything happen to you."

Bradley didn't get a chance to say anything else to him because a group of panicked students raced between them, jostling her as they passed. Donovan was lost in the chaos, but Bradley figured he could take care of himself fine on his own. She stumbled farther into the room, desperately searching for the people she loved. She located Beau first.

He was still fighting the group of vampires, but he now had Ashton assisting him. They seemed to be handling themselves okay, slowly wading through toward the dance floor.

Bradley's eyes found Dulapet in her search for Camden.

While Jordan Craven was preoccupied with Camden, Dulapet ordered one of the vampires to hand him his next victim. Dulapet pointed to Carl, a student in Bradley's English class.

The vampire pushed Carl forward, and without a moment's hesitation, Dulapet shoved his sword deep into Carl's gut. He twisted the sword to cause more pain before he viciously ripped it out.

Carl stood gaping at him in stunned silence before he collapsed to his knees. His hands went to his bleeding abdomen, his fingers automatically turning red as blood cascaded over them. "Why?" he whispered, and then fell to his face on the ground.

While Carl died at his feet, Dulapet licked at the blood

that trailed over the handle of his sword and down his fingers.

Bradley gave a terrified whimper. Her eyes shot in Beau's direction, but he was still caught up with the group of vampires. She searched for Donovan, finding him at the back of the room, fighting what looked to be another werewolf. Her eyes turned to Camden to find him crouching over Kristie in concern.

Kristie was quivering in terror, blue eyes as wide as saucers. She clutched the front of Camden's shirt in tiny fists, looking like a frightened deer.

While Camden was making sure Kristie wasn't hurt, Jordan Craven climbed to his feet. His nose was bloody and one of his eyes was practically swollen shut. He did not look happy to have been bested by Camden. His expression was one of complete loathing. He dabbed at his nose, and when his fingers came away covered in blood, he gave a holler of outrage. He lunged at Camden, seeking revenge for the injuries he'd received.

Camden reacted by instinct. He looked as if his body acted before his brain could even catch up to what he was doing. He thrust his stake up into Craven's approaching body to protect himself.

Craven's momentum drove him onto the stake. The piece of wood sunk into his torso about where his heart would be. He clutched at his chest in utter surprise. Rolling away from Camden, he stayed on his knees, gripping the edge of the stake that protruded from his body. He left the stake lodged inside himself, probably because removing it would only make him bleed out quicker. Blood began to seep from around the jagged piece of wood, staining Craven's shirt crimson. "You've ruined everything," he accused. "You and that bitch."

Camden climbed to his feet, shock filling his eyes over the realization that he'd just stabbed another human being.

Bradley watched frozen in horror as Craven pulled a gun from the inside pocket of his jacket and pointed the barrel in Camden's direction. Before anyone had time to react, Jordan pulled the trigger. The sound of the weapon firing echoed off the walls of the gymnasium.

Camden's eyes widened as the bullet slammed into his chest. He stumbled backwards with the force of the impact.

When staggering back, he put himself in Dulapet's reach.

Dulapet grabbed him from behind, and with a vicious jerk, he snapped Camden's neck.

Camden fell to the ground at Dulapet's feet, his wide, un-seeing eyes matching those of the other dead that littered the floor.

"Camden!" Bradley screamed. She sunk to her knees in shock, unable to look away from her dead friend. Her shoulders began to shake with gut wrenching sobs. As she cried in mourning, a shadow fell over her prone form.

"Are you ready to die just like your little friend?" a deep, cruel voice asked.

Bradley looked up through a curtain of her hair at one of Craven's vampires.

The vampire was shifting eagerly from foot to foot. He licked his fangs as his eyes skimmed enthusiastically over her body.

Lowering her head, Bradley closed her eyes, squeezing back her tears. There would be time to cry later. Right now, she had to keep others from suffering the same horrible fate as her best friend.

Using more self-control than she knew she possessed, she concentrated her efforts on one goal. She silently mouthed words under her breath, picturing two giant fire-balls in the palms of her hands. She pictured them burning bright and hot, though in her mind, she was exempt from their damage. She threw all her anger, hate, and remorse into her magical fireballs, and she believed. She believed with all her heart that she could burn the vampire in front of her into nothing more than ash.

Slowly, Bradley opened her eyes to find her hands glowing bright, fire dancing along her fingers. Raising her head, she stared up at the vampire with pitiless eyes. "No, you're the one that's about to die."

The vampire's eyes flicked to the fireballs and widened in alarm.

"Beau's right," she said softly. "No mercy. You've shown us none." With a flick of her wrist, Bradley sent one of the fireballs in the vampire's direction. She flinched as he caught fire, still unable to be okay with causing someone's death, but she had to do this. For Camden, she had to fight. She had to avenge his death. She had to fight to keep anyone else from dying.

A female vampire had stepped in Bradley's direction, her face full of puzzlement. "What the-"

Trying not to think closely on what she was doing, Bradley flicked the second fireball in the woman's direction.

The woman gave a shriek as the fire lit her hair. She beat at herself, trying to put the flames out, but the otherworldly fire spread too fast.

Before Bradley could even blink, the woman was engulfed in flames.

Not even pausing, Bradley pushed passed the burning pair of vampires, making a path to Camden. She knew there was nothing to be done for her friend, but she needed to go to him anyway.

Another vampire stepped into her way, and Bradley hit him with a large, and even hotter, fireball that had immediately filled her hand the instant the last one had been thrown.

As she did, Beau broke through the group of vampires. He'd gotten free just in time to see his girlfriend incinerate one of their foes. His eyes widened in surprise at her suddenly pitiless demeanor.

Meeting Beau's eyes was the hardest thing Bradley had ever done. Taking her grief out on their enemies had kept her from falling apart. Now, staring into his eyes, she was forced to come to terms with the realization that her best friend in the world was dead. Clenching her jaw to keep from crying, she gave a helpless look in Dulapet's direction, more precisely at Camden's body at his feet.

Beau's gaze followed hers, and when they landed on Camden, he gave a holler of rage. Without another look at Bradley, he stormed in Dulapet's direction.

Dulapet had been watching, a pleased expression on his face at their obvious remorse. "Beauregard Channing. You killed me once," he hissed out. "Now I return the favor."

Bradley watched in horror as the two of them began a fight that they meant to end in death. She'd already lost her best friend to Dulapet. She couldn't lose Beau too. Her legs trembling, Bradley stumbled past Jordan Craven's prone form.

Jordan's eyes were wide and staring, his body surrounded by a puddle of his own blood. Camden had killed him.

Bradley felt a rush of satisfaction at that. Jordan Craven had gotten exactly what he deserved. She couldn't dredge up one ounce of pity for a man so corrupt and wicked that he would sacrifice the lives of countless others for a measly bit of power. She brushed past Craven's body without a second glance, more intent on getting to Camden. Upon reaching her best friend, she collapsed to her knees next to him.

Kristie was sitting by Camden's side, tears running down her cheeks. "He saved me," she cried. "And that man just shot him. He was only trying to protect me."

Bradley's vision swam as liquid began to pool in her eyes. "Damn it, Camden," she accused, angry tears cascading down her cheeks. "Why did you have to go and be a hero?" As inconsolable as she felt at the moment, she was filled with pride at his selfless act. Her breath shuddering with a sob, Bradley looked up for Beau, concern filling her eyes at the thought of losing him as well. She was surprised to see that he had somehow managed to get Dulapet's sword and was brandishing it at its owner.

Beau was still as could be, waiting for Dulapet to make a move. "You know why I'm going to beat you again?" he asked. Without waiting for an answer, he continued. "It's because I've got something worth fighting for. I've got people I care about whose lives hang in the balance."

Dulapet's upper lip curled back in a sneer. "You're weak." He circled slowly around Beau, looking for an opening. "I'm going to kill you in front of your girlfriend, and then I'm going to torture her. She's going to die knowing that you couldn't protect her." Obviously hoping that statement would cause Beau to falter, Dulapet lunged at his adversary, a stake aimed at his heart.

Beau faltered, but only for a moment. He regained his senses just before the stake reached him. As Dulapet leapt forward, Beau ducked under his arm and moved out of the way. With precise aim, he swung the sword in his hands upward.

The blade connected with Dulapet's upper right arm. It sliced through skin and bone, severing the entire appendage. The stake in Dulapet's hand clattered to the ground as the arm fell lifelessly away from his body. Dulapet gave a feral hiss of anger and pain, his fangs dripping with spittle.

"You're not going to touch her," Beau said, his voice serene and sure of his statement. As wild as Dulapet looked, Beau looked that much calmer.

Composing himself, Dulapet straightened his shoulders to stand at his full height. He stared confidently at Beau, a smug grin quirking his lips. He ignored his bleeding stump, not seeming concerned over the loss of his arm. A dark, callous laugh emitted from his throat, and he said, "You have no idea the things we're going to do to her before I personally end her life. I'm going to make your lover my toy. I'm going to pass her around to each and every one of my men. Finally, when she's beaten beyond recognition and cursing you with everything in her heart, when she loathes you with every part of her being, I will end her life. She'll beg me for it."

Beau's face filled with outrage. He tightened his grip on the sword in his hands, a growl coming from deep within his chest. He shifted on his feet, his shoulders tense with anticipation.

Out of the corner of her eye, Bradley saw a flicker in the shadows to Beau's left. Her heart leapt into her throat as a figure crept around to circle behind Beau.

It was a vampire, one of Dulapet's. He was creeping up behind Beau, weapon in hand.

The words stuck in her throat for a moment, and Bradley feared that she wouldn't be able to notify her lover of the danger that was approaching. Finally, she managed to strangle out a warning scream. "Beau, behind you!"

Beau spun just as the vampire charged. He barely managed to block the incoming stake with his forearm. It glanced off his arm, tearing through his shirt and digging a ragged scratch through his skin. As the stake slid away, still gripped in the vampire's hand, Beau grabbed the vampire's wrist with his left hand and awkwardly spun the stake back into its owner's body.

Dulapet used this distraction to his advantage. From the waistband of his slacks, he pulled out a silver knife. He gripped it firmly in his hand, and when Beau turned back around to face him, he drove it through his enemy's chest.

Beau's body jerked at the impact of the knife slamming into his body, but he dealt with the agony that tore through him. Gritting his teeth against the pain, he swung Dulapet's sword around into its owner's throat.

The blade cleaved clean through Dulapet's neck. The vampire's own momentum drove the weapon straight through. The head separated from the body and hit the ground, turning end over end.

Bradley watched, feeling almost detached from the situation as Dulapet's severed head rolled in her direction. It had barely come to a stop in front of her before it disintegrated into dust. She had a hard time feeling anything but relief at his death.

As Dulapet's body hit the floor, Beau dropped to his knees. His hand went to the hilt of the knife sticking from his torso.

Stumbling to her feet, Bradley raced to Beau's side. She sunk down next to him, a sob escaping her at the sight of intense pain in his expression. "Beau..." She touched his arm gently, and then her hands slid to his face. She cradled his cheeks in her hands as tears streamed down her face. "Look what he did to you."

"I'm fine, Bella," Beau soothed. "I'm going to be all right." Steeling himself against the pain, Beau gripped the handle of the knife and wrenched it from his chest. He couldn't help the holler that ripped from his throat as the blade tore its way back out of his flesh.

The relief was nearly instantaneous, and he let the knife fall from his hand to clatter to the floor. At this moment, he needed his hands free. Reaching out, he cupped Bradley's face in his palms. His mouth lowered over hers, and he kissed her with a desperate passion. His lips moved hungrily against hers while his fingers touched her face as if checking to make sure she was really still alive. He tasted her salty tears, and his heart ached at knowing the cause of her suffering. "I'm so sorry," he whispered into her mouth. "I'm so sorry I couldn't save him."

Bradley's tears came harder at his apology. "It wasn't your fault. There wasn't anything we could have done..."

Beau pulled her into a tight hug. He tucked her head under his chin and rocked her protectively against his body. "That doesn't mean I'm not sorry," he whispered into her hair.

Overcome with emotion, Bradley sobbed into his shoulder, clinging to him as if he were a lifeline. The front of her shirt began to dampen with his blood, but she didn't care. She never wanted him to let go.

Beau held her, stroking her hair and whispering softly into her ear for as long as he could allow himself. He never wanted to let her out of his arms again, but they were still in danger. The remaining vampires were unorganized with all of their leadership gone, which might make them panic and do something stupid. He knew he was needed.

Finally, when he knew he couldn't procrastinate any longer, he whispered against her ear, "I need to help Donovan and Ashton round up the last of Craven's men. We can leave the few human followers of his for the police, so they have someone to point the finger at when they get here. It shouldn't take me long. With Craven dead, they will be disorganized."

Bradley nodded, feeling numb as Beau kissed her forehead, then untangled himself from her tight grasp.

He gave her one last, gentle kiss. "I will be back as soon as possible." With regret in his eyes, he turned and walked off into the chaos of a frightened crowd.

Without Beau holding her, Bradley felt cold. She felt weak and exhausted. Her heart felt as if it had a giant hole in it due to Camden's death. Sighing sadly, Bradley couldn't stop her eyes from going to her friend's body. The giant bloodstain on the front of his shirt made her stomach turn. Camden hadn't deserved to die like this. He was a good person and a loyal friend.

Kristie was still sitting by his side, tears streaming silently down her face. Camden had finally gotten her attention, but it had been too late.

"Why did this have to happen?" Kristie whispered as Bradley approached. She grabbed Camden's hand and went to pull it into her lap. Halfway there, she gave a startled gasp and dropped his hand, shaking hers in the air. "Ouch," she complained. "He's holding something sharp."

Bradley caught a flash of silver and her heart began racing in excitement. "No way," she whispered, almost hating to hope. Dropping to her knees next to Camden, Bradley pried his hand off the item he was clenching in his fist. Upon seeing it, she sat back with a gasp.

In Camden's palm sat her grandmother's necklace, a necklace that had the power to raise the dead. Somehow,

Camden had managed to get it from Craven, probably when he'd been pounding the other man's face into a bloody pulp.

"Camden, you're a genius," Bradley gushed. Gingerly taking the necklace from him, she put it around her neck, letting the silver pentagram hang between her breasts.

"That's pretty and all, but do you really think this is appropriate?" Kristie asked uncertainly. "You're stealing from a dead guy."

"Shh!" Bradley hissed. Closing her eyes, she placed a hand against Camden's chest, trying to ignore the wet feeling of blood. She let her palm rest above his heart. With her other hand, she touched the necklace, envisioning the power it held inside it.

"What are you doing?" Kristie asked, leaning over Camden to see, her waist length hair tickling Bradley's hand.

Peeking one eye open, Bradley hissed, "Shh!" Narrowing that eye, she added, "And sit back. You're getting blood in your hair."

With a look of horror, Kristie sat back, fingering her pretty, blond locks.

Able to concentrate again, Bradley closed her eye. "Don't talk," she warned Kristie. "Just be quiet."

Slowly, Bradley began talking up her own confidence. She was a witch. Just like her grandmother had been. She'd created balls of fire. She could do *this*. And she had the necklace to enhance her power. It could be done.

Digging her fingers into Camden's shirt just above his heart, Bradley ordered, "Beat." She drew on the necklace, envisioning its power running through her and into Camden. "Beat," she repeated.

Sliding her hand down a little, she took a guess at where his lungs would be. "Breathe!" she demanded. "Damn it, Camden! Breathe!"

Kristie shifted uncomfortably on the ground. "You're starting to scare me," she murmured. "You're, like, totally creepy right now."

Ignoring Kristie, Bradley pressed her palm against Camden's chest right above his heart and yelled, "Live, damn it!" Suddenly, Camden's pulse fluttered under Bradley's hand. She gave a sob of disbelief and pressed harder into his chest. "Breathe! Damn it. Just breathe, Cam. Please, please, breathe."

And then he was coughing.

Bradley gave an incredulous laugh that quickly turned into a sob.

With a groan, Camden propped himself up on his elbows. "I feel like I just got hit by a truck," he complained, rubbing his head with an expression of discomfort on his face. "What happened?"

Bradley threw herself at him, wrapping her arms around his neck to give him a big hug.

He laughed, patting her back. "What's gotten you so emotional?" he asked, struggling to a sitting position.

As Bradley moved back to give Camden some room, Kristie threw herself at him next. "You saved me! You saved me, and then they killed you, but she..." She waved vaguely in Bradley's direction. "...brought you back to life. She's, like, a witch doctor or something. It's actually kind of disturbing." With that, she pressed her lips forcefully to Camden's.

Camden jumped in surprise, but it didn't take him long to relax into Kristie's kiss. He responded to her in absolute delight for a long moment before what she was saying sunk in. Pulling back slightly, he looked at Bradley, his expression questioning. "I was dead?"

Bradley nodded, her stomach in knots. "Yeah."

Camden sat in silence for a moment, pondering this, before shrugging. "Cool," he said, taking the news of his death in stride. Turning back to Kristie, he gave her what he liked to call his "puppy dog eyes". "Could you do that thing with your lips again?" he requested. He pointed to his own mouth. "Right about in this region?"

Kristie nodded with a smile. "You're my hero," she gushed as her lips descended on his.

Bradley glanced away, giving them a little privacy. As she sat back, her eyes landed on Beau.

He stood frozen, his eyes wide in shock. "Bradley!" he growled, voice tinged in anger.

She blinked at Beau in surprise as he stormed over. She yelped when he grabbed her elbow and yanked her to her feet. "Beau, what-"

"What in the world were you thinking?" he hissed in her ear as he pulled her a few feet away.

"What are you freaking out about?" Bradley asked, yanking her arm free from his grip.

"You used the necklace," he came back heatedly. "The whole reason I was after it was to avoid just that, and it's been used twice in one night. I've never seen such irresponsible behavior before in my life..." He trailed off, too angry to even continue.

Bradley's mouth fell open in disbelief. Was Beau mad that she'd brought Camden back to life? "I didn't use it to hurt anyone," she argued in her own defense, upset at his disapproval. "I was using it for good. I'm not going to gain any power by bringing Camden back from the dead."

Beau sighed. He ran his hands over his face, realizing that she didn't fully understand what she'd just done. "Bradley, the few times this necklace was used, the people revived came back different. What came back wasn't entirely human."

Eyes widening, Bradley spun to look at her best friend.

Camden seemed so happy, so harmless as he continued to con kisses out of Kristie. He was laughing and his expression was one of bliss.

Turning back to Beau, Bradley gave him a look of concern. "Will he be okay?"

Beau shrugged in reply. "Don't know. You took a gamble with his soul." He paused, his eyes on Camden. "You made the right choice," he said softly.

Relief flooded through her, and she stared up at him with wide, hopeful eyes. "Did I?"

Beau pulled her in against his side. Leaning down to kiss her forehead, he whispered against her skin, "We'll just have to keep a really close eye on him the next couple of months, make sure he's normal."

Bradley's eyes lit up in happiness. "The next couple months? That means you're sticking around then?"

"I told you that I wanted to be with you. Stopping Craven and Dulapet doesn't change that."

"I was hoping you wouldn't change your mind," she said in relief. Her eyes showed just how concerned she'd been that Beau might walk out of her life now that her dilemma had been settled.

"Honey," Beau said, wrapping her tightly in his arms, "I saw you flinging those fireballs around. Do you think I want to risk scorning you? I'd have to be crazy."

She smiled proudly at the mention of her newfound ability. Before she could comment, though, Beau was nudging her toward an exit.

"We gotta go," he instructed under his breath. On Bradley's confused look, he nodded behind her.

Policemen had finally arrived and were attempting to secure the area. Behind them, reporters were trying to push their way into the building.

"We otherworldly types like to lay low," Beau said quietly. "Let's sneak out the back, shall we?" He motioned toward a tiny emergency exit along the back wall that, at the moment, Ashton and Donovan were slipping through.

As Beau started in the direction of the exit, Bradley followed after him. Just as they reached it, she glanced back to see Kristie dragging a reporter in Camden's direction.

"He's a hero!" Kristie gushed. "He saved my life. I love this man."

With a laugh, Bradley followed Beau out of the building. "I guess we'll have to meet up with Camden later."

Epilogue

Four days later, Bradley and Beau sat in the same diner they'd had their original "date" in. Bradley was stirring her straw around in her milkshake, glancing thoughtfully at Beau. "So, now that we're an official couple, are you going to turn me into a vampire?" she asked casually.

Beau quirked an eyebrow, but responded, "I don't intend to let you grow old and die on me, but I believe we've got awhile to discuss it." He gave her an amused smile. "We should let you get a little closer to twenty-eight so our age difference doesn't freak your brother out so much."

Bradley laughed. "When he finds out I've been turned into a vampire, he's going to have some bigger issues to worry about than our age difference." She laughed again. "He thought eight years was bad. I wonder what he's going to do when he discovers it's closer to four hundred."

"He would lock Bradley up and never let her out if he knew that you were a vampire," Camden's voice informed Beau from behind them.

Bradley gave him a big smile as he slid into the seat across from her and Beau.

Camden tugged Kristie down next to him, sliding across the bench to give her room. He slung his arm proudly over the blonde's shoulders, grinning like mad.

Kristie was too busy giving Bradley a serious look to notice that Camden was showing her off. "Locking children up is not good parenting," she chastised, voice thick with disappointment.

"It's her brother," Camden corrected.

"Well, it's not good...brothering," Kristie said, rectifying her earlier statement. Pleased with her advice, she bounced happily in her seat.

Beau couldn't help but give her artificial breasts a wary look.

Unable to help herself, Bradley asked, "Kristie...so...what happened to Carter? I thought you two were getting serious."

Camden gave Bradley a dirty look, which she chose to ignore.

Kristie's nose scrunched in displeasure. "You were right. He kissed like a fish." Spinning in her seat to face Camden, she patted him on the face a little roughly. "Not like Camden here. He kisses like a warrior." Biting her lip, she gave him a private smile. "He does other activities like a Greek god," she breathed.

Camden's face flushed in embarrassment, but his expression was one of pride.

"Are we talking about the strawberry syrup scenario?" Beau asked offhandedly.

Camden blushed even darker and waved Beau off. "Shh! That was spoken in confidence, and it's a little early..."

Kristie leaned over and whispered in Camden's ear, giggling as she did.

"Dear God," he breathed on a groan.

At that moment, Adrian and Katie walked unexpectedly up to the table, saving everyone from hearing anything else Kristie had planned to share.

Bradley was grateful for the distraction from Camden's apparently very active sex life, even if it meant Beau was about to be under the microscope.

"Funny running into you guys," Adrian said, voice bright with genuine pleasure, though his eyes turned a little unfriendly when they landed on Beau. Apparently, their truce was a shaky one that was easily forgotten when the mood arose to be antagonistic.

Katie gave Bradley an apologetic look. *Sorry,* she mouthed.

Unperturbed by Adrian's less than friendly greeting, Beau gave him a dazzling smile. "It's *great* running into you. We were just meeting a couple of my friends, Donovan and Ashton, for a late dinner, but you are welcome to join us."

Katie started to decline the offer, but Adrian cut her off. "Don't mind if we do," he said, pulling a chair up right next to Beau.

Sorry, Katie mouthed again.

Bradley gave her an understanding smile. Protective older brothers. There was nothing that could be done about them.

Adrian waited only a moment before giving Camden a big, open, friendly smile. "You're quite the hero I hear. The newspapers have been loving you."

Kristie patted Camden's hand affectionately. "That's because he's like a knight, a very sexy, masculine knight."

Adrian's eyebrows rose in amusement. "Okay..." he said slowly. Shaking his head at the idea of Camden being sexy, he turned to Beau. "Didn't hear anything about *you* in the papers. Where were you, off on another super important history adventure?"

Beau opened his mouth to say something Bradley knew her brother wouldn't appreciate, so she cut him off. "I was running late. We weren't there yet. It was my fault."

Beau frowned at the loss of an opportunity to make Adrian squirm, but didn't say anything to contradict Bradley's explanation.

Kristie's eyes lit with the realization that they were lying, and she opened her mouth to comment.

Before she could say anything, Camden began frantically whispering in her ear.

"Oh," she whispered back, loud enough to be heard by anyone at the table willing to listen. "He doesn't know about the vampire thing. I guess it makes sense to lie to him then."

Bradley gave a yipping noise of protest and tried to distract her brother. "So!" she cried, trying to drown out Kristie's voice. "What have *you* been up to lately?"

Beau gave Camden a silent, questioning look as he suddenly realized that Kristie knew he was a vampire. Camden had mentioned it around her earlier, but it hadn't sunk in until just now. He received a guilty shrug in response from the kid.

Bradley tried to ignore them, instead concentrating on her brother.

"I can tell you one thing," Adrian said with a note of superiority to his voice. "I haven't been on some Indiana Jones, historian, wild goose chase. Some of us have matured with age."

Bradley smiled at the wicked look behind Beau's eyes as

he thought of what snappy comeback he would use. Things were pretty much back to normal if her brother and Beau were back to their "friendly competition". That is if dating a vampire could be considered normal.

Silently thinking of blazing heat, Bradley pictured her hand containing the smoldering warmth of fire in her palm. Reaching over, she placed her palm on Beau's thigh.

"Well, good for you, Mr.—" Beau broke off with a hiss at the sudden hot tingle on his leg. He glanced over at Bradley, who mouthed, *Be nice.*

Beau sent her a fiery look of desire before turning back to Adrian. "Good for you," he said, trying for honesty. "It's not a bad thing to..." He glanced at Bradley and broke into a devil-ish smirk before turning back to Adrian. "...be completely boring before the age of thirty," he couldn't help but jab.

Bradley rolled her eyes with a laugh. She glanced at Camden to see what he thought of Beau and Adrian's antics. She swore for a second that his eyes were glowing a blazing red. Blinking in surprise, she found his eyes to be their normal green.

They were sparkling in delight as Camden laughed at Adrian's look of annoyance.

Bradley shook her head to clear it, figuring it was just her mind playing tricks on her because she was so concerned about his trip back to the living. That thought made her laugh. Okay, maybe her life was back to being *un*-normal, but she wouldn't trade a single thing about it.

About the Author

Melissa Hosack lives near Pittsburgh, Pennsylvania with her husband Jeremy and their four pets: Duke, Edge, Eddie, and Leia. She writes a monthly short story column titled *Frequent Flyer* for a government newspaper and had a short story, *More Bark Than Bite*, published by Mystic Moon Press in September of 2008.